Last Stop

on

Desolation Ridge

A NOVEL

by

Peter G. Pollak

ISBN: 0985036621

ISBN-13: 9780985036621

Acknowledgements

This is a work of fiction. Any resemblance to actual persons, organizations or places should be understood in that context.

I owe a debt of gratitude to a number of people who helped bring this book to fruition including Sonja Hutchinson who critiqued early drafts and Rita Pollak, Steven Pollak, Jo Ann Izzo Bussman and Claudia Gisondi Reed who found numerous typos and helped make the book better than it would otherwise have been with their comments and feedback. Jude Ferraro, not only proof-read, but put up with my running commentary on the book's progress.

I am extremely fortunate to have had the assistance of Kelly Mullen of *InVision Studios* whose design skills informed the development and production of the cover. Michael Bagnardi contributed the cover illustration.

None of the above is responsible for any deficiencies that may remain in the story or its presentation. Despite my diligent effort to ferret out typos, some may exist. If you come across what you think may be a typo (or any other mistake), you are welcome to call it to my attention.

Reviews on Amazon, Goodreads and other websites help authors gain visibility. Thank you in advance to any reader who takes the time to share her or his views on those and/or other websites.

Comments can be sent to me via my website: **www.petergpollak.com**.

Peter G. Pollak, January, 2013

"That might work in theory, Craig," Everett Lipton replied, "but they've got cameras on all those bridges now. No one has explained how I'm supposed to pull that off without someone seeing me doing it."

The African American gentleman stepped forward. "I have a suggestion."

"Okay," Zander said. "What would you have us do with him?"

"I had a nephew who tried to blackmail me when I wouldn't give him a job he wanted managing one of my clinics. He was a drug addict and would have brought the feds down on me so fast, I'd have turned white."

Lipton and Zander laughed.

"So how did you handle him?" Lipton asked.

"I sent him to a mental hospital in the Adirondacks and he's still there."

"You mean you had him committed?" Harkness asked.

"No. My sister would have gone nuts if I'd gone through legal channels. No, I made it look like he committed himself voluntarily to deal with his drug problem. I drove him up to the hospital. It costs me a few bucks each year for them to keep him there, but it's worth it."

"I like it," Zander said.

"Hey, it looks like he's coming around," Harkness said, pointing to where Logan Gifford was trying to stand up.

Something was preventing him from getting out of the chair. There was a strap across his chest and his arms were tied behind his back. "Mr. Zander. Please. I have to use the bathroom."

Zander looked at Lipton. The security chief nodded his approval. "He should be okay by the time he gets back."

"Okay, Logan," Zander said. "These men will go with you to make sure you get back here safely. There's some business we need to take care of."

The men escorted Gifford to the men's room. They stood behind him while he used the urinal. "May I?" he said pointing to the sink. They move aside. He washed his hands, then splashed some water on his face.

"I feel strange," he said aloud.

He couldn't explain why. He looked at himself in the mirror. He looked much like he always did––an all-too-average looking businessman in a navy blue suit with a white shirt and a red patterned tie.

There were times when Logan was on the train going home from work when he felt invisible. He'd sit there worrying whether he'd be able to find his car among all those cars that looked so much alike and then whether he'd remember the way to the street where he lived and whether he'd be able to pick out his house from all those look-alike houses. What if he pulled into the driveway of what he thought was his house and some other man who looked just like him was getting out of a car that looked just like his car and kissed a woman at the front door who looked just like his wife?

"Let's go," one of the men said.

He looked for the towel dispenser. "You can go back," he told the man. "I don't feel well. I think I'll go home."

The larger of the two men shook his head. "I don't think so, Mr. Gifford." He was built like a football lineman and he wasn't smiling. The other one was taller, but thinner. He had a crew cut and a nasty scar on the side of his nose that matched the nasty look he was giving Logan. The men grabbed Logan, lifted him off his feet, and shoved him out of the bathroom.

"Help. Someone help me," Logan screamed, but the entire floor was empty. He remembered wondering why he had been told to come to a meeting at this location. Everett Lipton had met him in the lobby and escorted him to the 17th floor. When they got off the elevator, the entire floor was vacant. When he asked what was going on, Lipton told him he'd find out when the rest of the people arrived.

The men forcibly ushered Logan back into the conference room and dumped him in the chair in front of the camera. They secured a strap around his chest, but left his hands free.

"Craig," Logan said, looking at his brother-in-law who stood in the corner looking out the window. "Tell them to let me go home."

Craig Harkness came over and stood in front of Logan. "They will, Mac, as soon as you do what Mr. Zander wants you to do."

Zander came over and handed Logan a sheet of paper. "Logan, listen to me. Are you paying attention?"

Logan nodded.

"This will all be over as soon as you memorize and read this statement for the camera."

Logan took the paper on which was one paragraph typed in all capital letters.

> I, LOGAN GIFFORD, BEING OF SOUND MIND, FREELY ADMIT THAT I KNOWINGLY AND FRAUDULENTLY OVERCHARGED THE UNITED STATES GOVERNMENT FOR TEKRAM'S SERVICES SO THAT I COULD EMBEZZLE THAT MONEY FROM MY COMPANY.
>
> I APOLOGIZE TO MY FAMILY AND TO THOSE WHO PUT THEIR FAITH IN ME. WHAT I DID WAS WRONG. NO ONE ELSE AT TEKRAM WAS AWARE OF MY DECEIT. I CAN'T BEAR THE THOUGHT OF GOING TO JAIL.
>
> GOOD-BYE, DEBBIE. FOREGIVE ME IF YOU CAN.

He read it a second time. "What does this mean, Mr. Zander? I didn't negotiate that contract. In fact, I was the one who told you the numbers were way off."

"And, that's what you planned to tell the Congressional Ethics Committee next Thursday, right?"

"Of course. It's the truth."

Zander laughed. "If you do that, then Congressman West here and I will be on our way to jail. That just can't happen. It's either you or me, Logan, and it's not going to be me."

That's who the third man was. Logan remembered being introduced to Congressman West several months ago when he'd been asked to analyze a bid proposal. The New York City Congressman chaired the subcommittee of the House Committee on Appropriations that had jurisdiction over Tekram's bid.

Logan read the statement a second time. "No way. I'm not going to do this."

"Logan," Everett Lipton interjected. "Do you see what's on that TV screen? That's a live feed of your house. Some nasty people are in the bushes outside your house right now waiting for me to give them the go-ahead to do some nasty things to your wife and children. If you don't do what Mr. Zander is asking, I'm going to tell them to have a field day."

"Craig," Logan said, appealing to his brother-in-law "Help me. They're talking about your sister and your nieces."

"Half-sister," Harkness replied. "Look, Logan, there's nothing I can do. You're the only one who can save them."

Logan tried to take it all in. "I don't believe this. If this is someone's idea of a joke, it's gone way beyond funny."

Zander moved close, inches from Logan's face. "It's no joke, and if you don't wise up Everett is going to call those men and tell them to do their worst."

Logan tried to fight back the tears. "If I do what you say, what will happen to me?"

"After you read the statement, you will disappear," Zander replied. "The government will find evidence of your crimes. Tekram Industries will survive and Congressman West will continue his illustrious career. Your sacrifice will save Tekram and the hundreds of people who work for us. If we were to let you spill the beans, I would go to jail, the company would go out of business, our investors, including Craig here, would lose their money, and everyone who works for us--all nine hundred--would lose their jobs."

Whatever Lipton had injected in him had almost worn off. Logan was beginning to understand his predicament. "You can't fool me into thinking you care about those people. All you care about is that you won't have to go to jail."

Zander shook his head. "Whatever. The fact is that I'm not going to jail. I'm going to cooperate with Congress and come out smelling like a rose while your name will go down in history as another greedy accountant."

Logan tried again to clear his head. None of this made any sense to him. Maybe he could appeal to their sense of decency. "Why me?"

"Let me answer that," Lipton replied. "You're the logical choice. You manage all of the data––the contracts, the bank accounts and you are the only person with the ability to hide things from upper management. Plus, you're a pussy––constantly watching what the rest of us are doing, trying to make us into a goodie-goodie like yourself. Me, I'm enjoying seeing you take one for the team."

"Well, I'm not doing it. I don't believe you'd do those things you said to innocent people just to save your own skin."

Zander stared at Logan for a minute. "You leave me no choice," he said. He nodded to Lipton. The security chief picked up his cell phone.

"Put it on speaker," Zander said, "so Mr. *Goodie Two-Shoes* can hear both ends of the conversation."

"707 here."

"This is 101," Lipton said. "Are you in position?"

"Affirmative."

"The home security system is off-line?"

"Affirmative. We cancelled their contract last week. I tested it when we got here. No response."

"Excellent. Here are your instructions. There are three occupants in the house at 11745 West Bright Woods Lane: a woman and two female children––ages 3 and 6.

You are to terminate all three without remorse. You and your men may take your pleasure with the woman before you terminate her. Do you understand my instructions?"

"Affirmative."

"Also, make sure that the camera records the entire procedure so that her husband can watch what you do to them."

"Got it."

"Over and out."

"Stop," Logan yelled. "You're crazy. You can't mean that. Stop him."

Zander shook his head. "Too late, Logan."

Logan tried to turn his head away so he couldn't see the TV screen. He struggled to get out of his seat, but the restraints were too tight. "Help. Help. Someone. Help."

"Hold his head," Lipton said to his men, "and, if he tries to close his eyes, you have my permission to pry them open."

The person holding the camera started moving towards the front of the house. Logan heard him talking to a man dressed as a mail carrier. "Ring the door bell. Keep the woman occupied until I confirm that we're inside. Then push your way into the house and lock the front door." The man nodded and walked towards the front of the house.

The man with the camera panned the house. Logan saw two men dressed in black with hoods over their heads with holes for their eyes and nose waiting at the edge of the woods. The men moved in a crouch towards the back of the house. One of them held a crow bar while the other carried a large heavy gym bag.

Logan kicked out trying to connect with the legs of Everett Lipton who was watching the monitor. Craig Harkness pushed Lipton aside. "Read the statement,"

Harkness said. "Please, Logan. Agree to what they're asking."

Logan watched the man with a crowbar approach the back door of his half-a-million dollar house. He inserted an end into the door and gave it a yank. The door gave way.

"Okay," Logan screamed. "Okay. I'll do it. I'll do it. I'll do it."

Harkness looked back at Zander. Zander smiled. Almost reluctantly, he nodded to Lipton.

Lipton picked up his phone.

"101 here. Abort," Lipton said, "Abort. Remain in position."

"Abort. Affirmative."

The person with the crow bar turned and moved away from the house. The camera showed the two men moving behind the bushes on either side of the back door.

Zander turned to Logan. "Ready?"

Logan's heart beat so rapidly he feared he would have a heart attack. The sweat poured down the back of his neck. His hand shook as he held up the script and tried to memorize it. Finally, he nodded, indicating that he was ready to read what he was certain amounted to a death sentence--his own.

Chapter One

(Wednesday October 5, 2005)

It was almost three in the morning, but Paul Gustafsson, head of security at Stoner Sanitarium, knew the call had to be made. It took more than a dozen rings before Dr. Plentikov answered his phone. "We've got a problem, boss," Gustafsson said.

Plentikov didn't respond right away. Gustafsson imagined the man's blood pressure rising. "Talk," Plentikov said finally.

Gustafsson hesitated. He knew he was doing the right thing in waking Plentikov, but also knew he was about to get his head handed to him. "Our John Doe is missing."

"How can that be?" Plentikov yelled into the phone. "How could someone we keep under the strictest security go missing?"

Gustafsson's mouth felt dry. "He can't have gotten far. He's on foot, in pajamas, wearing flip-flops."

"Then find him," Plentikov said enunciating every syllable. "Call me as soon as you have him. In fact, call me every 30 minutes. And, by the way, Mr. Gustafsson, tomorrow someone is going to lose his job. So you'd better get to the bottom of this if you don't want that someone to be you!"

The phone line went dead. Plentikov's reaction had been pretty much what Gustafsson had expected. Thinking about it, he wouldn't be too upset if he were the one who got fired. He was ready to cash in the job anyway. He wanted to move back south. Living in the Adirondacks was too much like living in northern Minnesota where he grew up. He hated the weather, he hated the people who liked living there and he hated the job.

Right now, however, he had to find a missing patient.

An hour earlier, Gustafsson was the one who had been woken up. The caller was Terry Brower, the night duty officer.

"Room 4A is empty," Brower had stated.

"I know that," Gustafsson replied testily. "Don't you read your duty report?"

"What? Was he released? I must have missed that," Brower mumbled.

"No, you idiot. He was moved upstairs to room 8C because of tomorrow's state inspection," Gustafsson said. "Now don't bother me again unless it's a real emergency."

"Okay. Sorry, boss."

"Oh, Brower?"

"Yeah, boss."

"You might not recognize him. Jimmy gave him a haircut today and trimmed his beard."

"Okay boss. Sorry."

Gustafsson had finally fallen asleep when the phone rang again. He looked at his bedside clock. Forty-five minutes had gone by.

"Now what?" he said picking up the phone.

"He's not there either," Brower stated.

"What do you mean he's not there?" Gustafsson demanded.

"He's not in room 8C or any other room," Brower repeated, "He's gone."

"If I find out you've woken me up for nothing..." He left the specifics of the threat unspoken. There'd be time enough for that later.

When he arrived at the facility, it didn't take Gustafsson long to discover that Brower was right. The patient was not in the room where he'd been moved earlier that day. The two men checked the entire building before Gustafsson accepted the fact that he'd have to inform Plentikov.

Gustafsson told Brower to begin a thorough search of the facility grounds. Despite its remote location, Stoner Sanitarium was fenced in. There were only a couple of possibilities. Unlikely, but it was possible that someone had left a gate open and the patient had gotten lost in the woods. The more likely possibility was that he walked the quarter mile driveway to the main road and was on the state highway. From there, he would not be difficult to follow since he was on foot and there were no houses in either direction for more than a mile. Gustafsson wasn't worried that the escapee could get far on his own. The danger was that someone driving by might pick him up. However remote that possibility, there'd be hell to pay if it happened--especially if the local sheriff or state police were contacted.

"This man is being kept here for his own protection," Plentikov told the staff when the patient he called John Doe arrived almost two years ago. When a nurse asked why he was kept in a padded cell, Plentikov had replied, "It's because of his history of violence. He doesn't look dangerous I'll grant you, but you have to watch out for the quiet ones. We're keeping him in the padded room for his protection and for yours as well."

While that answer may not have satisfied the nurses and orderlies, it was good enough for Paul Gustafsson. He didn't care why someone was at Stoner. His job was to keep patients in and outsiders out.

Gustafsson woke up the two other men in his security unit and told them to get their butts up to the facility ASAP. When they arrived, he assigned them to walk the main road on foot with flashlights and walkie-talkies.

An hour passed. Gustafsson knew he'd better call Plentikov. "No luck thus far."

Plentikov swore, then was silent for a few seconds. "When you do find him, dress him in his street clothes. They're in the storage room. Put him in the unmarked van. Then call me."

Plentikov must be worried about team from the State of New York Health Department that was due the next morning to inspect the facility. Although Stoner was private, the Health Department had jurisdiction over such things as staff credentials and the storage and dispensation of controlled substances. Gustafsson suspected Plentikov would do anything to avoid having to report that a patient had escaped his facility.

Dr. Plentikov had not shown any concern about the inspection--except for the confinement of his John Doe in the padded cell. That's why he ordered the man moved to the second floor and had several crates of supplies moved into the isolation room after the patient's bed had also been removed.

"If they ask about that room, tell them we only use it for emergencies," Plentikov instructed his staff.

Gustafsson found Brower wandering around in the back of the building. "Any sign of him?"

"Nothing. Want me to get my dog?"

"There's not enough time. Keep looking." Gustafsson didn't trust Brower. He had to consider the possibility that he'd let the patient loose intentionally. He could be angling for a reward for finding him or just wanting to screw things up.

Gustafsson headed back to the main building. It was almost time to check in with Plentikov. His walkie-talkie beeped. It was one of his men. "I've got him. He's sitting on the side of the road. Says he's thirsty. I told him you'd bring him some water. He says he wants a sandwich, too."

Gustafsson breathed a sigh of relief. "Good job, Hayes. I'll be there in ten minutes."

Gustafsson called Plentikov. "Got him."

"Good. Now listen to me very carefully," Plentikov said. "This may turn out for the best. Don't bring him back to the facility. Get him dressed in his street clothes like I said. No coat. Just pants, shirt and shoes; then strap him in the van and drive south. When you get to Meadow Lake, take Route 62 South. About fifteen miles from Meadow Lake, there's a stretch where there's a deep gully on the eastern side of the road. Do you know where I'm talking about? The locals call it 'Desolation Ridge'."

"Oh, yeah. I know where that is," Gustafsson said. "Nice view of nothing."

"Good. When you get there, remove him from the van and push him over the guardrail into the deepest part of the gully."

Gustafsson wasn't sure he heard right. "Push him over the guardrail?"

"That's what I said."

"He'll never survive. It's miles from anywhere."

Gustafsson heard Plentikov laugh. "That's the idea, Gustafsson."

Chapter Two

(Thursday, October 6, 2005)

As soon as he recognized the spot where he planned to photograph the morning sunrise, Bernard Floer pulled his van onto the shoulder. He spotted the location several weeks ago when driving back from shooting a historic Adirondack camp and promised himself that he'd come back before winter. He'd been attracted by the fact you couldn't see any signs of civilization. The view from the side of the road looked like it must have looked hundreds of years ago when Native Americans hunted for deer and fished the stream that meandered through the desolate valley.

Bernard did a u-turn and parked on the western shoulder facing south. Sunrise was just minutes away. He hurried out of the car and crossed the road, flashlight in hand, looking for the right place to set up his camera. Having made his decision, he went back to his van and unloaded his equipment.

Minutes later his camera was set up on as level a footing as he could find, without getting too close to the steep gully on the other side of the guardrail. As the sun began to peak over the horizon, he checked the camera's settings, then pushed the button for the camera to snap pictures automatically every five seconds.

Floer stopped the camera when the sun fully cleared the horizon. The job done, he took a deep breath of fresh

Adirondack air. He felt exhilarated. How many times had he driven to a spot he'd picked out for its unique beauty only to be thwarted by weather conditions, equipment problems or other calamities, such as the farmer who wanted to be paid to allow Floer to capture a sunset over his cornfield?

That morning everything had turned out perfect. He had caught the sunlight shining through the mist that rose off the small river. The sky, the thin cloud cover, everything had been perfect.

Satisfied, he began to pack up his equipment.

Not surprisingly, no cars had passed in either direction since he'd arrived. Route 62 was one of the least trafficked roads in the entire Adirondacks. Yet, in his opinion, it was one of the most photogenic highways in the Eastern United States. He hoped he'd captured a view he could use in his next book of outdoor photography––maybe even one suitable for the cover.

As he checked to make sure he hadn't left anything behind, Bernard heard a vehicle approaching. A large truck––the kind lumber companies use to haul their loads from the Adirondacks to the mills in the Mohawk Valley––was bearing down on him. The driver must have seen Floer because he beeped his horn twice and steered to the center of the highway.

After the truck had gone by, Bernard was about to cross over to his car when he heard something that made him hesitate. It sounded like a moan. How could that be? It must have been the wind on the guardrail. But no, there it was again. He looked around.

"Who's there?" he called. No answer.

He walked over to the gully and looked down. It was too dark to see the bottom. Maybe it came from the other side? He went back to the side of the road where his SUV was parked. He listened for a few seconds, but couldn't hear anything. I must be dreaming he thought.

The scene on that side of the road caught his eye. He selected one of his cameras and took some shots of the mist coming off the stream that crossed under the highway.

Satisfied he put his camera away and started to get into his car. Then, remembering times when he'd left things at a shoot, he crossed back over to the eastern side of the road to make sure he hadn't lost something--a lens cover or a screw from the tri-pod assembly.

Satisfied that he had everything, Bernard took another look at the valley in front of him. He congratulated himself on a nice job--even if he had to get up at four in the morning to do it. As a reward he thought about the breakfast he'd enjoy at the small diner half an hour back towards home. What? It sounded like someone had called 'help.' He peered over the edge of the guardrail. It was still dark below.

"Hello," he called tentatively.

"Here," came a faint answer.

He peered into the black nothingness. "Is someone there? Do you need help?"

"Yes," came the faint reply.

Maybe he saw something. Was the dark form wedged between two large boulders a person?

"I think I see you. Wave your arm."

It was slight, but something moved. Bernard looked around to see if there was any way that he could climb down the steep embankment. Even if he could, how could he bring someone who was injured back up?

"Hold on. I'll call for help," he yelled down.

His cellphone was in the center console of his van. He ran across the road, threw open the car door and yanked the phone out of its case. 9-1-1. Nothing. No bars. No service. "Damn."

He ran back to the other side. "There's no cell service here," he yelled down at the motionless body. "I'll have to drive to get help. Hang in there. I'll be back as soon as I can."

He ran to his car, jammed the key into the ignition. That poor person, lying down there! How did he get there? Bernard stomped on the gas.

He didn't know how far he'd have to drive before he reached a house that looked occupied. Most of the homes on the road were summer camps or hunting cabins. It would take half an hour before he reached the diner in Spruce Lake where he'd planned to stop for breakfast––twenty minutes if he stepped on it.

He checked his watch. It was five of seven. Although it was beginning to get lighter, he still needed his headlights. He drove as fast as he could on the winding road, sliding into the other lane on the curves. Rounding a bend, he saw a house with its front porch light on. Did someone live there? He pulled into the driveway, got out of the car, knocked loudly on the front door.

Nothing. He knocked again harder. He heard someone on the other side. "What do you want?"

"There's a man hurt bad back up the road," Bernard yelled through the door. "Can I use your phone to call for help?"

"Hurt? Where?"

"North about ten minutes. Please, I need to call 911."

"We don't got 911," the man said, still not opening the door.

"What do you have then?"

"Volunteer rescue."

"They'll do," Bernard said. "Please hurry. I told the man I'd come right back."

The door opened. On the other side stood a short heavy-set man with sparse hair and a bulbous nose wearing a plaid shirt and suspenders over grey pants. He led Bernard into his kitchen, where a phone hung from the wall.

"What's the number for rescue?"

"It's on the wall," the man said pointing to a bunch of numbers scribbled on the wall next to the phone.

Bernard read down the list. He dialed the number next to the word rescue spelled with a q. "I've got an emergency to report," he said as soon as the call was answered.

After answering what seems like an endless series of questions, he was told to drive back to the location and to leave his headlights flashing so that the rescue crew would know where to stop.

He hung up the phone. "They're sending the rescue people."

"If there was no car, how did the man get in the gully?" the man asked.

"I don't know," Bernard replied, "but I'd better get going. I told the person I'd be right back."

When Bernard got back to the spot where he'd taken the sunrise photos, he was so anxious to find out if the man was still alive that he almost forgot to start his flashers. He had a terrible feeling that the man might have died because he hadn't tried to rescue him himself.

He got out of his car, grabbed his flashlight and went over to the edge of the road. He almost wished no one was there, that it had all been his imagination while half fearing that someone was down there, hurt, possibly dead. He could see more clearly now as the sun had risen in the sky. A body lay twisted at the bottom of the gully. His stomach turned.

"I'm back," he called down. "Help is on the way."

There was no answer.

"Did you hear me?" Bernard called. "Help is on the way."

Chapter Three

(Saturday, October 8, 2005)

He was trying to run. People were chasing him. They were getting closer. He had to reach the door in front of him. His legs wouldn't respond. He began to panic. Why couldn't he move?

Someone was shaking his shoulder. "It's okay. You're okay." He opened his eyes. A woman in a nurse's uniform stood over him.

"What--?" He tried to sit up. "Where--?"

"You must have been dreaming," the nurse said. "You were calling out."

The feeling of uncontrolled fear still coursed through his nervous system. His legs were cramping. He twisted uncomfortably.

"Try to lie still," the nurse said. "You're strapped in. You don't want to pull out your IV's."

"My legs," he whispered. "I can't move them."

"Your right leg is in a cast."

A cast? The nurse gave him a sympathetic smile. *Where was he? How had he gotten there?*

"You've had an accident. It's natural to feel panicky when you wake up," she said as if reading his mind. "Take a few deep, slow breaths. The feeling will lessen."

He tried to do as she suggested, but his chest hurt. "Where am I?"

"Nathan Littauer Hospital in Gloversville."

"What happened to me? I can't remember."

The nurse was looking at a monitor next to his bed. "Don't try to talk. Just breathe. Deep breaths."

He tried to do what she told him. Breathing deeply made him conscious that his midsection was wrapped tightly. His head hurt. He hurt all over.

"Just breathe," she said again.

He began to feel drowsy. He closed his eyes.

Denise Richardson went back to the nurses' station. "What was going on in there?" asked Monica Sanders, one of the nurses with whom Denise shared ICU night duty.

"He woke up in a panic," she said. "I upped his dosages a bit and he went back to sleep. The State Police will be here to talk to him in the morning."

Chapter Four

(Sunday, October 9, 2005)

He was in deep water, but he couldn't kick his legs. He was starting to go under. He yelled for help. He tried to reach out his arms, but they wouldn't move. He called again. Air. He needed air. Someone was shaking his shoulder. He opened his eyes.

A large nurse looked down at him. "Bad dream?"

Was he dreaming?

She touched his arm. "Are you okay?"

Was he?

The nurse checked the monitors. "Hungry?" she asked.

Did he feel hungry? He was always hungry. He nodded.

"You'll get some food right after the doctor sees you."

He tried to fight down a feeling of panic. He didn't want to see the doctor. Not until he could remember. He wanted to sit up, but he was strapped down except his right arm. He lifted it up and saw a cast half way up the arm. His head ached. *What happened to me?*

A man in a white coat came into the room. "Good morning. I'm Doctor Bhatt."

The friendly nurse was back also. She smiled at him.

The man relaxed a bit. "What…what happened?"

"That's what we'd like to know," the doctor replied. "But don't try to tell me what you remember now. Someone from the State Police will be here shortly to talk to you. Are you hungry?"

He nodded.

"Nurse will bring you some cereal that you can eat through a straw. How do you feel all in all?"

"Terrible."

"We're giving you some pain medication," the doctor said. "Let us know if it's not working."

The feeling of panic rose up again in his throat. He began to sweat. The doctor looked at the monitors.

"Take it easy now, sir. There's nothing to get upset about. You need to keep your blood pressure from rising. Can you do that for me?"

The man shook his head, surprised to learn that he could move it from side to side.

"Try," the doctor told him. "Practice. Deep, slow breaths."

The man had heard that instruction before, but he couldn't remember when. He tried to take a deep breath. He felt it in his ribs. "Ow."

"You made a mess of your rib cage," the doctor said placing his hand on the man's left arm. "It's going to feel a bit uncomfortable for a while, but the day will come when you'll be able to walk out of here on your own feet. Whenever it hurts, think about the day when you'll be going home."

Home? Where was home? The man tried to think. What came to mind was a dark room with no windows. Why couldn't he remember?

Chapter Five

(Same Day)

The man woke up. He was almost happy to see that he was in the same bed in the same room. A different nurse came in to tell him that he had visitors. A minute later two people in police uniforms came into the room--a woman who had a severe look on her face followed by a younger man. The woman kept her trooper's hat on.

"You're awake, I see," the woman said. "I assume he can hear me," she said to the nurse.

"He can and he can speak," the nurse answered.

"Good. My name is Sergeant Jerzinski," the policewoman said, enunciating each word. "I am here to ask you a few questions, but I need you to consent to my recording this interview."

"Why?" he asked.

"To help you," Sgt. Jerzinski answered.

"Help me?"

She showed him her miniature tape recorder. "To make sure we get all of the relevant information."

"I guess," the man said.

"You can't guess," Jerzinski said. "You have to say 'I agree.'"

Should he? Why not? "I agree."

"Good." She placed the recorder on the table next to the bed. "Let's begin with your name."

The man was silent.

"Are you sure he can hear me?" Sgt. Jerzinski asked the nurse.

"I think so," the nurse replied. "Ask him again."

"What is your name?" Jerzinski said, enunciating each word even more slowly.

"I can't remember," the man said.

Sgt. Jerzinski looked annoyed.

"You don't know your name or maybe you don't want to tell me? If that's the case, we'll find out sooner or later. You might as well tell me now."

"I truly can't remember," the man said.

"All right. If that's the way you want to do it," Sgt. Jerzinski said. "We'll come back to that. Do you know where you are?"

"In a hospital?"

"True, but where?"

"She told me," he said nodding at the nurse. "Gloversville, I think."

"Is that your answer?"

The man nodded.

"Please don't nod your head," Sgt. Jerzinski said. "Either say 'yes' or 'no'. Okay?"

The man nodded.

Sgt. Jerzinski looked annoyed. "Do you know what happened to you?"

"No," the man said. "Can I have some water?"

The nurse slipped in front of Sergeant Jerzinski, took a red plastic glass with a plastic cover off the table and placed it so that the man could sip from the straw.

"Thank you," the man said.

The other officer, who had been standing at the foot of the bed, sat down in a chair so that the man could no longer see him.

Peter G. Pollak

"We'd like to know how you ended up in the bottom of a gully on a desolate road in the middle of the Adirondacks. Can you explain that?" Jerzinski said.

"I can't remember," the man said.

"You can't remember?"

The patient shook his head; then recalling the Sergeant's instructions, said, "No. I can't remember."

Jerzinski looked at her partner. "Okay. Try this. Where are you from?"

The man thought for a minute and then shook his head. "I don't know. I can't remember."

"Where do you live?"

The patient shook his head again. "I don't know."

"Are you telling me the truth?" Sgt. Jerzinski asked.

Just then Doctor Bhatt came into the room. "So sorry I'm late," he said. "How are we feeling this afternoon?"

"Lousy."

"Doctor," the nurse said, "this is Sergeant Jerzinski and Officer Collins."

"Pleased to meet you," the doctor said. "Are you getting the answers you wanted?"

"No," Sgt. Jerzinski replied. "He's not giving us anything––his name, where he's from or what happened to him."

"Really," Dr. Bhatt said. "Maybe I can help."

"You're welcome to try," Sgt. Jerzinski stated.

Dr. Bhatt moved to the right side of the bed. "I know you're in a lot of pain," he said. "But it's important that we help these nice police officers find out what happened to you."

The man nodded. "I'm trying."

"Excellent," Dr. Bhatt said. "But maybe you're trying too hard. Now just close your eyes and tell me what comes to your mind."

The man closed his eyes. He heard a babble of voices. Some were angry; some seemed familiar, but he could not put a name to them.

"I hear voices," he said.

"What are they saying?" the doctor asked.

"They're angry. I want to get away from them."

"Are you seeing anything else?"

The man closed his eyes again.

"A door."

"What kind of door?"

"Metal," the man said.

"What else can you tell us about the door?"

"It's grey."

"Is there a window in the door?"

The patient thought. "I think so."

"Good," Dr. Bhatt said. "Go to the window and look out."

The man shook his head. "It's covered."

"Can you tell me anything else about the room?"

"No," the man replied. "Wait. There's a mattress on the floor."

"Good. What else?"

"That's all."

"How did you get in that room?"

"I don't know. I keep telling you. I don't know."

Dr. Bhatt looked over at the monitor that displayed the patient's blood pressure. "Relax. There's no reason to get upset. You'll remember more as time goes by. I'm afraid you're not going to learn very much today, Sergeant."

"I can see that," she replied.

"This man has been in a terrible accident. He seems to have received one or more severe blows to the head as well as broken bones. It may be some time before he remembers much."

"Days? Weeks?"

"I can't really say," Dr. Bhatt replied. "Maybe tomorrow; maybe next week. We can't predict these things. As my professor used to say, 'the brain has a mind of its own.'"

The sergeant stopped the tape recorder. "Call us when he starts to remember something," she said. "Here's my card."

Peter G. Pollak

Chapter Six

(Tuesday, October 11, 2005)

He was awake. An orderly was helping the friendly nurse change the bandages around his midsection. Every movement hurt. He tried not to complain because he knew they were trying to be gentle. When they were done, the nurse tucked the blankets around him.

"Would you like to sit up a little? You could watch TV for a while."

The man nodded.

"How many days have I been here?" he asked.

"Let's see," the nurse said. She went over to the chart. "You came in on a Thursday and now it's Tuesday. Five days."

"It's hard for me to keep track."

"I understand. Here's the remote. Do you want me to show you how to use it?"

The man nodded. The nurse demonstrated and handed him the remote.

"What month is it?"

"October."

The man's head moved slightly. "Are you remembering something?" the nurse asked.

"I thought so . . . for a second. I like October. Leaves turn. Halloween."

"That's right," she said. "Halloween."

"And football."

"Push this button when you want to turn the TV off," she said showing him where the power switch was on the remote. "Oh, we need to give you a name. What would you like us to call you?"

"A name?"

"Yes, we can't keep calling you John Doe."

" But, I can't remember my name."

"Maybe you have a nickname, like Bud or Al or Nick."

The man shook his head. "Mac," he said suddenly. "I like Mac."

"Okay, Mac. I'm Denise. Nice to meet you."

"Nice to meet you, Denise. I just wish it were under better circumstances."

Denise laughed. "That's the spirit."

The man smiled, but then he remembered he was in a hospital with broken bones in his arm, chest and leg and that he had no idea what happened to put him there. He didn't fight back the tears.

The nurse patted him on the shoulder.

Stop crying he said to himself. *You could be dead.*

Chapter Seven

(Thursday October 13, 2005)

The first parking spot he could find in the visitor's lot was a good distance from the hospital entrance, but NYS State Police Lieutenant William Sheridan didn't mind. It was one of those sunny October days that made you think winter would never come.

While waiting for Dr. Bhatt, Sheridan reviewed Sergeant Jerzinski's report on the man found at the bottom of a roadside gully deep in the Adirondacks. She wrote that the patient was suffering from a form of amnesia and was unable to answer basic questions. She also wrote that it was possible that he was hiding what he knew, either to protect himself or loved ones.

As an investigator in the Criminal Investigation Division of the New York State Police, William Sheridan was used to dealing with victims of organized crime activity, which is why his boss had decided to send him up to Gloversville. He looked forward to questioning the mystery patient.

Dr. Bhatt invited him into his office. The room was neat, exactly what Sheridan would have expected from Dr. Bhatt's personal appearance. The doctor, who looked to be in his fifties, wore a brown herringbone jacket and subdued tie. He spoke with a distinct accent, but he must be highly regarded in Gloversville as his was a corner office.

The patient was still listed in serious condition ten days after he'd been rescued Dr. Bhatt stated. "He remembers almost nothing of his past and he has no concrete knowledge of the events that caused his injuries."

"Have you learned anything new since Sergeant Jerzinski's visit?" Sheridan asked.

"Yes. We discovered that he was in very poor health even before his accident," Dr. Bhatt stated.

"How do you mean?"

"His weight is very low relative to his height and from his blood work we detected severe deficiencies in vitamins C and D as well as iron and other minerals."

"What would cause that?" Sheridan asked.

"An extremely poor diet over a considerable period of time."

"How long? Six months?"

"Yes––possibly even longer."

Sheridan wrote that down in his notebook. "I may want to ask you some more questions after I talk to him, but I'm ready to see the patient."

Sheridan followed Dr. Bhatt to the patient's room. Dr. Bhatt explained that a nurse had awakened the patient a few minutes earlier for his 10 A.M. medications. His bed had been elevated slightly so that he could see his visitors.

The man barely responded to Dr. Bhatt's greeting. He had a far-away look and gauntness that seemed to confirm Dr. Bhatt's conclusion that the man had not been in good health prior to the accident.

Sheridan introduced himself. "I've been told they're calling you 'Mac?'"

The man nodded.

"Why do you think that is? Could it be your name?"

He shrugged. "I don't know."

"Do you think it's your first name or last name?"

"I'm not even sure it's my name," he replied.

"So you still don't remember your real name?" Sheridan asked.

The man shook his head. "I've tried different names––John, William, Michael, George––none of them seem right."

"Can you remember anything about how you ended up in that gully?"

The man shook his head.

"Please vocalize your answers," Sheridan said, pointing to the tape recorder he had placed next to the bed.

"I have no idea how I got there," the patient replied.

"Do you remember anything about being in the gully?"

The man thought for a moment. "I remember a horn blast. Then came the pain. My leg, my wrist, and my head…everything hurt. I couldn't move and I couldn't tell where I was or remember how I got there."

"Then what happened?"

"I tried calling for help and someone answered."

"That would be the photographer?"

The man nodded. "Thank god someone heard me. Otherwise, I'd be dead."

"And, how are they treating you here?" Sheridan asked.

"Very nice…Dr. Bhatt here and the nurses…everyone."

"We're just doing our job," Dr. Bhatt said. "Your job is to get better. That will be our reward."

The man managed a thin smile.

"I'm going to ask you a series of questions," Sheridan said. "Tell me the first thing that comes to mind. Okay?"

The man nodded.

"Who is the President of the United States?"

"I know that because I've been watching the news," the man said.

"That's okay," Sheridan answered. "Tell me anyway."

"It's George Bush."

"What year is it?"

"I'm not sure. 2003 maybe?"

"Where were you born?"

The man thought. He shook his head. "I don't remember."

"What state did you grow up in?"

He thought for a moment. "Pennsylvania maybe. I really can't say."

"Did you attend college?"

The man's face brightened slightly. "I think so. That sounds right."

"Do you remember what you studied?"

"No."

"Chemistry?"

He shook his head.

"No to chemistry," Sheridan said. "How about English literature?"

"I don't think so."

"Mathematics?"

"Possibly."

"Art history?"

"No."

"Accounting?"

He paused. "Could be."

"History?"

"Maybe."

"Politics?"

"I just can't remember."

"That's okay," Sheridan said. "A few more questions. Are you married?"

"I think I am," he replied.

"Do you have children?"

"Hmm," he said. He frowned. "I feel like I have children."

"Yes, no, or you're not sure?"

"I'd say 'yes,'" the man answered.

"Are you left-handed?"

He lifted his left arm, which he had been forced to use to operate the TV remote and feed himself. "No."

"What sports did you play growing up?"

The man thought for a while. "No idea."

"What's your favorite baseball team?"

His face brightened again momentarily. "The Mets."

"Football?"

"The Jets."

"Not the Giants?"

"They're okay."

"Do you play golf?"

"Hmm. I might have tried it."

"Have you ever been outside the United States?"

"I'm not sure."

"Yes or no?"

The man thought. "I think I have, but I can't remember where."

"What do you see when I say outside the U.S.?"

"The ocean. Palm trees."

"Hawaii?"

"Could be."

"Europe?"

"Perhaps."

"*Parlez vous Francaise*?"

"Is that French?"

"You tell me," Sheridan said.

"It sounds like it."

"*Comment vous appelles*?"

"Sorry, I don't know what that means."

"*Lei parla italiano*?"

"That's Italian, right?"

"*Quanti anni hai*?"

"I don't what that means either."

"*¿Quantos anos tienes*?"

"How old am I? Is that Italian also?"

"No, it's Spanish," Sheridan said. "Next question: do you have any sisters?"

The man thought. "Maybe."

"How many?"

"Not sure."

"But at least one?"

"That sounds right."

"Do you have any brothers?"

"No, I don't think I do," he said quickly.

"Is your mother still alive?"

The frown re-appeared. "I'm pretty sure she's gone."

"Recently?"

"Perhaps. I don't know."

"Your father--is he still alive?"

"I don't have a feel for that."

"Do you have any sons?"

The man thought for a minute. "I don't think so."

"Any daughters?"

He nodded. "Yes, I believe so."

"How many?"

He shrugged. "Two?"

"Do you remember their names?"

He thought for a while. Something almost came, but then faded. He shook his head.

"Name someone you admire."

The man thought. "Jack Welch."

"Anyone else?"

"Clint Eastwood."

"Have you ever been arrested?"

After a second or two, the man shook his head. "No, I don't think so."

Sheridan made a note on his question sheet. "Which is worse–someone who sticks up someone on the street or someone who burglarizes a home?"

"They're both bad. I wouldn't want either to happen to me."

"Choose. Which is worse?"

"Robbery, I suppose."

"What about burglarizing someone's home or stealing from a business––which is worse?"

"You mean like shop-lifting?"

"No, like extortion or cooking the books."

The man hesitated. "Which is worse?"

"Correct," Sheridan replied.

"They're both wrong."

"Which is worse?"

"They're equally bad, aren't they?"

Sheridan made a note.

"Have you ever been in prison?"

"No…I don't think so."

"Have you ever been the victim of a crime?"

The man flinched––just slightly, but enough for Sheridan to notice. "I take it that is a 'yes'."

The man brought his right hand––the one with the cast on it––up to his face for a second. "I get a feeling that I have, but I can't say why." Dr. Bhatt noted a change in the man's heart rate, but didn't say anything to the investigator.

"What are you feeling right now?" Sheridan asked.

"Hurt, sad," the man said.

"Why?"

"I don't know. I just am."

"Okay. That's enough for today. I'm going to leave this tape recorder with you with a blank tape in it. Anytime you remember something about your past--a name, a place, an event--even if you don't think it's important, would you record it for me?"

The man nodded.

"If you'll do that, Mac, I promise we'll do our best to find out your name and all the rest--where your family is, what happened to you and why."

Chapter Eight

(Same Day)

Lt. Sheridan put a dollar bill in the coffee machine in the hall and punched in his selection. He purchased a package of peanut-butter crackers and sat down in the waiting area. Dr. Bhatt indicated he would only be a moment, but it had already been more than ten minutes since he'd gone into his office to take an "important" phone call.

Sheridan used the time to write down a few key words to help him remember the questions he wanted to ask the doctor.

"So, what do you think?" Bhatt asked when he finally invited Sheridan into his office.

"Very interesting," Sheridan admitted. "What's your take on your patient? Is he hiding something or telling the truth?"

"Hard to say with 100 percent confidence," Bhatt replied, "but when he says he doesn't remember his name or what happened to him, I believe he's telling the truth."

"What do you think happened to him?"

Bhatt shrugged, turning his palms up to the ceiling.

"Let me be more precise," Sheridan stated. "What do you think was the cause of his injuries? Was he beaten, hit by a car, or perhaps he was walking, tripped and fell into that gully?"

Bhatt shook his head. "Not beaten. The bruises were too irregular. The pattern suggests the likely cause was a fall."

"At the scene where he was found?"

"That would be the most logical conclusion. If he had been injured elsewhere and then moved to that location, in most instances any injuries caused by a beating could be distinguished from those caused by a fall."

"What about the memory loss--could that be the result of a fall from that height--approximately thirty feet?"

"I've been thinking about that," Bhatt said. "He would have had to hit his head very hard to suffer amnesia, and while he does show signs of having a concussion, I would have expected more damage to be associated with amnesia."

"Any other observations?"

"As I indicated, he was in a weakened condition prior to the fall. His body looks like he lost a considerable amount of weight, and his blood work showed serious iron and vitamin deficiencies."

"Again, your best guess as to the cause?"

"Extremely poor and limited diet."

"For how long?"

Bhatt shrugged again. "As I said before, at least six months--probably much longer."

Sheridan made a note on his pad. "Anything else?"

"He was examined soon after he came in by Dr. Chassen, the resident psychiatrist here at the hospital. Dr. Chassen says the patient shows symptoms which are consistent with sensory deprivation and that those symptoms exist apart from the effects of whatever caused his physical injuries."

"Sensory deprivation? Is that in the latest information you gave me?"

"Yes, it is."

"Good," Sheridan said. "I'll read it over and then contact Dr. Chassen if I have any questions. That's all for today, but I'd like to be notified if there are any changes in his condition, especially if he records anything in the tape recorder, no matter how insignificant it may seem."

"Of course," Dr. Bhatt answered.

Sheridan spent the hour drive back to Albany thinking about what he would put in his report. The patient's responses suggested that he studied accounting or mathematics. It was likely that he was married with one or two daughters. He may have been in some kind of confinement for six months or longer, but not in the United States since he had been subjected to conditions that were illegal in the U.S., even for the most hardened offender. If not prison or some other form of confinement, he must have been living under extreme circumstances.

Rather than put it in his written report, Sheridan decided it best to bring up the sensory deprivation theory in person when he met with his superior officer, Captain Anderson Falcone.

"The only situation which even remotely comes to

mind would be solitary confinement in a prison, but we can't find a match with his fingerprints to any crime database," Sheridan told Falcone. "That strongly suggests he hasn't been in any prison in this country."

"You're suggesting overseas?" Falcone asked.

"I suppose he could have been in prison in some foreign country where they might not have fed him well and kept him locked in the dark, but doesn't the FBI know about every American citizen who is being held in a prison overseas? If so, wouldn't this guy show up in some database?"

"Possibly. If he was fingerprinted in the U.S., he would, but he might not have been fingerprinted," Falcone said. "Sometimes people whose fingerprints are not in our system get arrested and imprisoned overseas."

"True," Sheridan said, "but wouldn't the FBI have some knowledge of that?"

"Possibly," Sheridan's boss replied. "What have your searches come up with?"

"Nothing. Absolutely nothing."

Falcone took a sip from his coffee mug. "Say he'd been in a foreign prison. Then how would he end up in a gully in a remote location in the Adirondacks?"

Sheridan nodded agreement. "Under no scenario that I can think of."

"What about Canada? Did we check with them?"

"We did," Sheridan replied. "Nothing that matches the information we have at the moment."

By the end of the meeting, Falcone had agreed with Sheridan's recommendation that he return to Gloversville to talk with the hospital psychiatrist.

Chapter Nine

(Monday, October 17, 2005)

Dr. Arnold Chassen was in his late-thirties or early forties. He was short, balding and overweight.

"I read your analysis, Dr. Chassen, and I find it fascinating," Lt. Sheridan stated in Chassen's office. "You suggest this man had experienced an extended period of sensory deprivation prior to his physical injuries?"

"That's correct," Chassen answered.

"How did you reach that conclusion?"

"Normal conditions of light, sound and/or movement can overload the brains of people who have suffered sensory deprivation. They find it hard to parse the information coming into their senses."

"Couldn't the brain injury that caused his amnesia result in the same condition?"

"Possibly, but not very likely. That's why I wrote that sensory deprivation was a distinct possibility, but not a certainty."

"From what I learned from the patient, I would have concluded that he led a pretty normal life prior to his injury. He thinks he attended college, was married, had children and held down a job. That's not the kind of life-style we'd associate with sensory deprivation."

"True. I can't explain the cause of my findings, and I may be wrong, but that's what came to mind when I examined him."

"Could some kind of physical illness produce similar symptoms?"

"Again, I'd have to say that's possible, but neither Dr. Bhatt nor I could find signs that he'd suffered from any illness that would correspond with his physical condition. His body shows no signs of previous surgeries and no signs of previous brain damage. That's why I suggested that something other than his fall contributed to his state of confusion and the slow response times he demonstrates to simple stimuli."

After meeting with Dr. Chassen, Sheridan decided to go back to talk to the patient. First, he stopped by the nurses' station to ask the nurse on duty whether she'd noticed any changes in the patient's behavior.

"His body is healing slowly," Mary Beth Howard informed Sheridan, "and he's able to stay awake for longer periods of time."

"What does he do with his time?"

"Right now, not much of anything," she replied. "He's not interested in daytime TV although the night nurse says he watches Wheel of Fortune and Jeopardy every night."

"Does he talk much?"

"When you ask him something, he'll answer, but he doesn't say anything unless we say something to him first."

"He still responds to 'Mac,' correct?"

"Yes," she answered. "He seems to like that name."

The patient opened his eyes when Sheridan entered his room. "How you feeling today, Mac?"

"Been better," the man replied.

"I'm sure," Sheridan said. He noticed a slight improvement in the man's pallor. "I have a couple of questions if you don't mind?"

The patient shrugged his shoulders.

"Why do you think this happened to you?" Sheridan asked.

The man seemed surprised by the question. It took him a while to answer. "I must have made God angry."

"Do you believe in God?" Sheridan asked.

"I don't know. I guess so."

"I'll name some religions. You tell me which one you think you might belong to, okay?"

The man nodded.

"Jewish?"

"No."

"Catholic?"

"No."

"Baptist?"

"No."

"Presbyterian?"

"Maybe."

"Unitarian?"

"No."

"Muslim?"

"Definitely not," the man said.

"What comes to mind when I say 'church service'?"

"Stained glass windows."

"Good," Sheridan said. "Did you jump into that gully on your own?"

"I've thought about that," the man replied, "but why would I? Someone must have thrown me down there."

"Who? Who would do that to you?"

"Someone who didn't like me. Someone who didn't want me to live."

"Okay," Sheridan replied. "So, let's try to figure out who that might have been."

The man laughed. "How are you going to do that?"

"Stay with me. I have a couple more questions for today. You said the other day you might have studied accounting in college. Do you still think that's correct?"

"I can't say for sure, but it sounds––how can I say it––familiar, whereas other fields like art or chemistry sound foreign."

"Okay. So thinking about accounting, do you think you might have worked for an accounting firm or as an accountant for a company?"

"I don't get any kind of read off that question," the man said.

"Okay, let's try a different approach," Sheridan said. "What is it that appeals to you about accounting?"

"It just sounds like something I know something about."

"Then you probably worked in that field."

"Could be."

"Do you think you were a boss, managing other people or you worked under someone else's supervision?"

"I don't know that I was anyone's boss, but perhaps that's because lying here in these casts I can't imagine bossing around a flea."

A sense of humor, Sheridan thought. A good sign.

Sheridan left a half an hour later. He understood Sgt. Jerzinski's frustration, but didn't agree with her conclusion that he was withholding information intentionally. Yet he was stumped. His advanced training, he told himself, should have given him more insight into the man's identity, but he had to admit that there were too many disparate facts in this case that didn't add up. A severely injured man is found in the middle of a remote part of the Adirondacks with no memory of how he got there. He shouldn't be hard to identify. He has characteristics of being a middle-class American. His speech pattern, for example, suggests such a background. Sheridan picked up verbal clues––from his vocabulary and pronunciation––that he spent time in downstate New York, New Jersey or Connecticut.

What about the possibility that he's some kind of foreign spy? But that didn't add up, unless perhaps his sponsor had some reason to want him dead.

That's the angle that intrigued Sheridan the most. He either attempted to commit suicide or someone wanted him dead. Thinking on those two options, the suicide angle didn't hold water. How did he get to that location and, if he drove himself, where was his car?

If someone wanted him dead, why not just shoot him and leave his body in the gully or hit him in the head a few times with a rock or stick him with a knife?

If he was pushed into that gully, the perpetrator didn't leave any evidence. There were tire marks on the side of the road, but the only ones they could match belonged to the photographer and the rescue squad vehicles.

The worst aspect of the case was that Sheridan didn't know where to go next. He was at a dead end unless the victim started to remember things. Hopefully that day would come soon.

Peter G. Pollak

Chapter Ten

(Wednesday, October 19, 2005)

The patient wasn't happy. That morning, hospital officials insisted that he adopt a name for purposes of applying for Medicaid. He didn't want to use some phony name. He wanted to know his real name. Why couldn't they figure out who he was from his fingerprints and dental impression?

Dr. Bhatt told the patient it was possible that he wouldn't recognize his name even if they told it to him. That didn't make the patient happy, but he had little choice but to accept the doctor's logic and go along with their request that he adopt a new name.

"You can always change it back when you remember your original name," Marsha Nestor, Vice President of Primary Care Services, told him.

The patient gave in. "Okay. I guess I'll use 'Mac.'"

"Is that your first name or your last name," Nestor asked.

"Good question."

"Medicaid is not going to accept an application with only one name on it. You decide––first or last?"

He had trouble choosing a last name. "You pick one," he told her.

"Okay. How about Johnson?"

Mac shrugged. "I guess that's okay."

Henceforth he was to be Mac Johnson. For better or worse he said to himself. A new name and it looked like a new life as well.

Mac had started physical therapy. It was not fun.

Getting out of the bed into a wheelchair and being asked to stand--even with bars to keep the weight off his bad leg--was difficult. That he had one arm in a cast didn't help, but Mac knew they were pushing him for his benefit. So he didn't complain.

Each day when he went back in his room, he looked forward to seeing the nurse named Denise Richardson whose shift started at 3 P.M. She was the one person whose visits he looked forward to.

While the other nurses were friendly for the most part, he felt that he was just another stop on their rounds. In Nurse Richardson's case, however, he genuinely felt that she had an interest in his welfare and she truly tried to help his emotional as well as physical health.

One afternoon she popped her head into his room. "You have a visitor."

"Not the state police again," groaned Mac.

"Nope. It's a surprise," Denise said. She used the remote to maneuver him into a sitting position. "How's that feel?"

"Fine. So, who is it?"

"You'll see," she replied. "He'll be here in a minute."

A minute later a strange man came into Mac's hospital room. He was about Mac's age, had a 60's style Beatles' haircut, though worn shorter than the Beatles. He wore a light green button-down shirt under tan sports jacket.

"Good morning. I'll bet you have no idea who I am."

"Should I?" Mac inquired.

"I suppose not. I'm Bernard Floer. I'm the man who found you."

Mac perked up. "How nice. They never told me your name. Just that a photographer found me."

"I'm the one."

"I guess I owe you my life. I don't know how I can ever repay you..."

"Just seeing you alive is thanks enough," Floer said. "I was so worried that help wouldn't come in time."

"I guess I was barely conscious."

Floer nodded. "You really had me scared."

"Thank you for coming to visit me. The nurse said it's a long drive for you?"

"Not that far. Plus, I'm used to it--driving long distances that is. How are they treating you?"

"As well as can be expected," Mac said.

"I see you're still in casts. How long do they stay on?"

"They tell me the one on the arm comes off soon, but the one on my leg will have to stay on a month or more."

"Still, you're alive."

Mac nodded. "In body."

"And, in mind," Floer said. "You seem to have all your faculties."

"Except memory."

Floer startled. "Except memory! You mean--"

"I mean I can't remember a thing that happened to me before the morning you found me."

"Nothing?"

"Not my name, not where I'm from and not how I got there in the first place."

"But the police, they should be able to figure it out--what with fingerprinting and dental records and all that."

"Not so far," the patient said. "Or at least they haven't told me if they have found something."

"I'm sure they would."

Mac thought for a minute. "I guess I'm feeling a little bit paranoid. After all, I doubt many people need to be rescued from the bottom of a gully off a poorly-traveled road in the middle of nowhere."

"I suppose you're right about that," Floer replied. "Still, they're sure to figure it out sooner or later. What about the doctors--what do they tell you?"

"They say they don't know. My memories could return tomorrow or they may never return."

"Damn," Floer said. "That's adding insult to injury."

"In spades," Mac said.

"So what do people call you?"

"That's another sore subject," the man said. "They made me pick a new name so that the hospital can apply to Medicaid to pay my bills."

"I guess you can understand their point of view. They must be spending a lot of money taking care of you."

"I do understand that part of it, but it still irks me that I can't remember my own name."

"Can you remember anything?"

"Stuff that's not about me. I can remember Ronald Reagan and Jimmy Carter. I can remember that Bill Gates founded Microsoft and I can remember that the Yankees beat the Mets in the World Series. Was that last year?"

"Hmmm. Let me think. I think that was three years ago. Can you remember anything else?"

"I think I had two daughters, but I can't remember their names." Tears came to his eyes.

"You can't blame yourself," Floer said. "It's not your fault that you can't remember."

"I guess you're right, but that's the rub, Mr. Floer--"

"Call me Bernard, please."

"That's the problem, Bernard. I feel I am responsible somehow. I feel like I did something that resulted in my being in this awful situation."

Peter G. Pollak

Chapter Eleven

(Tuesday, October 25, 2005)

Lawrence Zander told his secretary that he was not to be disturbed. He sat behind his desk waiting for Craig Harkness to fix himself a drink. Everett Lipton, Tekram's security chief, sat stoically in one of the large leather chairs in front of Zander's desk. Congressman Clarence West stood looking out the window sipping on an expensive Scotch. Zander was tempted to pour himself one, but he didn't want to delay hearing Harkness' report.

Harkness had refused to tell him anything over the phone.

"I take it you saw him?" Zander asked once Harkness had settled into a chair.

Harkness nodded. "I did. It's him. There's no doubt in my mind."

"Shit," Lipton said. He'd been the one who pushed for Harkness to travel to Gloversville to eyeball the man who had been rescued in the Adirondacks, arguing that it was possible Dr. Plentikov had pulled a bait and switch on them in order to get more of their money. Harkness, being Logan Gifford's brother-in-law, was the obvious choice to make the trip since he knew Logan the best and was not likely to confuse him with some derelict Plentikov found in a gutter.

"How close did you get? How does he look?" Zander asked.

"He's been moved out of ICU to general population, but he's in a private room. I pretended to be looking for some other patient. I opened his door. His eyes were closed. I left quickly because I didn't want him to see me. He has a beard, but there's no doubt in my mind that it's him."

"Okay. That answers that question," Lipton said. "What about his mental condition? What does he remember? Is he a threat to us?"

Harkness took a sip of his whiskey. "If he did remember things and started singing, wouldn't he be under police protection?"

"You may be right," Lipton said. "But--even if that's the case--that he is too injured to give them anything right now, what happens if he wakes up some morning and says, 'My name is Logan Gifford and I've got a story to tell?'"

"Of course," Zander said. "There's no question something has to be done about him now that we're certain it's him. The question is, what?"

"There's another question we need to ask ourselves," Lipton said. "Do we trust Dr. Plentikov?"

Zander looked over at Congressman West who had recommended they send Gifford to Stoner Sanitarium in the first place. West shrugged. Zander rubbed his hand over his face. "Do we have any choice?"

"Absolutely," Lipton said. "There are always options."

"Such as?"

"Such as we tell Plentikov 'thank you very much; your part of the deal is over' and we find someone to clean up his mess."

"What do you think, Congressman?" Zander asked.

"If Plentikov fucked up, I'd make him clean up his mess. As long as it can't be traced back to us, what's the worst that can happen?"

"Don't be naïve," Lipton said. "Of course it can be traced back to us. Do you think Plentikov is a fool? I've no doubt that he's got documentation in his desk drawer that makes it look like we're the bad guys and he's just an innocent doctor trying to help a patient."

Zander nodded. "Unfortunately, Everett's right, Congressman. We're wedded to Plentikov at the moment. So we need to decide if he's is capable of finishing the job."

"How do we assess that?" Craig Harkness asked. "We were led to believe that everything was going nicely. Then one day he calls you up and says, 'Your John Doe is missing and presumed dead.' Well, it turns out that presumed dead and being dead are two different things."

"What if we tell him we want him to finish the job and give him a deadline?" Zander asked.

Lipton raised his hand. "I'll go along with that for one reason and one reason only. We've got Paul Gustafsson to keep us informed. If he tells us that Plentikov is stalling or incapable of acting, we take over."

"That's a good point," Zander said. "So you'd better have a backup plan ready in case we need to move quickly."

"That's exactly what I intend on doing," Lipton replied.

Peter G. Pollak

Chapter Twelve

(Same Day)

Dr. Plentikov hung up the phone with more force than he'd intended. So what! They couldn't have noticed at the other end. Besides, he wasn't angry with them. In truth, there was no one he had a right to be angry with other than himself. His patient, who should be dead, had been rescued and, if he recovered even part of his memory after nearly two years of sensory deprivation and a starvation diet, they all might end up in prison.

It had taken a lot of persuasion, but Plentikov had convinced the men who had sent the man he knew as John Doe to his hospital to let him clean up the mess. This time there could be no loose ends.

Paul Gustafsson found Dr. Plentikov staring out the window. He didn't think the medical director's mind was on the view. "You wanted to see me, sir?"

Plentikov swiveled his chair around to the front. "Sit," he instructed. "You and I created this mess," the medical director said, "so you and I will have to clean it up."

"What mess is that?"

"John Doe survived."

"You're kidding! That's impossible."

Plentikov scowled. "I never kid and he's lying right now in a hospital bed down in Gloversville."

Gustafsson thought it was a little unfair of Dr. P to place any of the blame on him. He did what he'd been told to do, but he decided not to make a big deal out of it. He was well paid to do what he was told and he was interested in learning what Plentikov had in mind. "But how?"

"Some guy found him near death, but he survived. Fortunately, I have a contact there--a technician by the name of Flint--who I can rely on for information. He tells me the state police have been in to question the patient a couple of times but aren't getting much of out him. He can't remember his name or how he ended up in the ditch."

"That's good," Gustafsson said, "but what if he starts to remember things? Will this guy do the job for us?"

"I don't want him to do anything more than keep us informed. As soon as there's any indication that John Doe is starting to recover his memory, we have to be ready to act--and this time there can't be any loose ends."

Chapter Thirteen

(Friday, October 28, 2005)

Denise Richardson was worried about the patient known as Mac Johnson. While his broken bones and other injuries continued to heal, albeit slowly, his emotional state remained precarious. She looked in on him one afternoon in the beginning of her shift.

"Are you awake?" she asked. "I've brought you a present."

The patient, who has been napping, opened his eyes. She placed a vase with a single red rose in it on his bed stand. "It's all that I could afford," she said, "but your room is so drab. I guess I'm used to seeing flowers in most patients' rooms. I decided you needed something to brighten things up, even if it was only one rose."

"Why thank you," Mac said. "You didn't have to."

"Of course, I didn't, but I wanted to."

He smiled.

"So how's your day been?" Denise asked.

"Just terrific. I solved all the world's problems before lunch and have been napping ever since."

"That's the spirit," Denise replied. "When things look the worst, tell a joke."

"Trouble is, I don't know any jokes."

"Sure you do. I've got one. Did you hear about the hunter whose buddy keeled over with a heart attack?"

He shook his head.

"The hunter called 911 and the operator said, 'first, make sure he's dead.' So the hunter said, 'Just a minute.' The operator heard a loud bang. The hunter came back on the phone and said, 'now what?'"

Mac laughed so hard he started coughing. "Ouch. That hurts."

Denise gave him some water. "Sorry," she said.

"No, don't be," he said with a grin on his face. "That was funny."

"So, how are you spending your days?"

"Well, other than being tortured by the physical therapy team, I mostly spend my time wondering why the State Police haven't been able to figure out who I am."

"I'm sure they're still working on it."

He shrugged. "I guess so, but I keep thinking if they can figure out who I am maybe I'll start to remember my past. If not, where does that leave me? What am I going to do when I am well enough to leave the hospital? How am I going to live?"

"Those are very good questions and it's not too soon to start coming up with answers."

"How can I when I'm stuck here 24 hours a day?"

"I can help you get started. Have you met Connie Jenner, our staff psychologist? I'll ask her to come in to talk to you."

"I guess it won't hurt, but I'm thinking about practical problems like where will I live. I don't have a red cent to my name."

"Fulton County Social Services will help you until you're back on your feet. I'll ask someone to come in to start the paperwork."

Mac frowned. "That's welfare, right?"

"That's what people used to call it."

"I never thought I'd be on welfare."

Denise placed her hand on his. "There's no shame in it. All kinds of people make use of it and it's not permanent. When you find a job, you get taken off."

"I guess you're right. It's good to know that I'm not going to be homeless in the middle of winter."

"Maybe they can help you find a place to live."

"What about clothes?" Mac asked, "I don't have a pair of socks to my name."

"Yes, of course--you'll need clothes and the basic necessities for an apartment. It's likely they can provide most of that."

"That makes me feel a little better," Mac said.

"I'll contact them tomorrow before I come to work."

"There's still one thing that bothers me," the patient said.

"What's that?"

"It's something the state police officer said. Either I threw myself into that ditch on my own or someone pushed me. That means there's a good chance there's someone out there who wants me dead."

"You're worried that they'll find you and try again?"

"Exactly."

"You should discuss that with the state police officer the next time he returns. Maybe he'll able to help you in some way...like witness protection."

"If he ever comes back."

Denise stood up. "You have his card, right?"

Mac looked at the bedside table. "Someplace here, I think."

"Then call him."

"I guess so. But then there's the other possibility."

"What's that?"

"Suicide."

"You think that's what happened?"

"I don't know," he said, "but what if my memory returns and I find out that I did something horrible and wanted to end my life for a good reason. Maybe that's why I can't remember. Maybe my mind is protecting me."

"But Mac, you don't know that you did something that drove you to suicide. We can't live our lives worrying about something that may or may not be true."

"That's good advice, but lying here all day with nothing to do, it's hard to stop myself from thinking about it."

She adjusted his blankets. "Have you tried reading? We have a pretty decent library."

"The librarian has been here, but I wasn't in the mood."

"Just try. If you don't like the first book, try a different one."

"Okay. I don't know how I can ever thank you."

"That's my job, Mac."

"You seem to put more of yourself into your job than some of the other nurses."

"We all do what we can," she said. "Some of us have more capacity for helping than others. I'd better get back to the nurses' station now."

Mac watched her leave. He always felt better whenever she was in his room. But when she left, he immediately felt depressed. You've got to be more positive, he told himself. At least you won't be sent out into the world with no place to go.

He was almost asleep when he started thinking about his situation. Which was worse--the possibility that he'd tried to commit suicide or that someone had tried to kill him? If he didn't throw himself down into that gully, that meant there was someone out there who wanted him dead. Who could that be and why?

If he couldn't remember who it was that wanted him dead, they just wait until he was out of the hospital and finish the job! He was helpless.

Peter G. Pollak

Chapter Fourteen

(Tuesday November 1, 2005)

Paul Gustafsson pulled his sedan around in back of the farmhouse as he'd been instructed so it wouldn't be visible from the road. The barn door was wide open suggesting that C. J. Flint and his girlfriend didn't keep any animals in it. It was a typical damp early November day--gray and raw. The back door to the house opened up. A man waved for Gustafsson to come inside.

"You must be Gustafsson," the man said. "I'm C.J." He was thin, had wispy hair and the worst handlebar mustache Paul had ever seen.

"Going to work or getting off?" Gustafsson asked stepping inside the house.

"Just got up. Going in an hour."

"Where's MacVean?"

"She'll be here shortly," Flint replied. "I'm brewing some coffee."

"Love some," Gustafsson said.

Flint led him into the kitchen. Dirty dishes filled the sink and cigarette butts overflowed the ashtray on the table.

"Mind?" Flint said, taking a cigarette out of the pack from his shirt pocket.

"Suit yourself," Gustafsson replied pulling out a chair.

Flint was pouring the coffee when Gustafsson heard a car pull into the back yard. The driver revved the engine a couple of times and then shut it off.

Donna MacVean was the first woman to serve on the Gloversville Police Department. It took five years and a lawsuit to get the job. Since then, she'd made up for lost time. It was well known that MacVean was on the take. She was particularly tight with a former cop named Ralph Quinn who ran the main book-making operation in Fulton and Montgomery counties.

"Money talks," Dr. Plentikov told Gustafsson, "and Donna listens."

MacVean came into the house. Her uniform enhanced her solid build. The slips of blond hair that escaped her hat couldn't hide her square jaw and steely cold eyes. "Gustafsson?" she said sticking out her gloved hand.

"That's me," Paul answered, standing to shake her hand.

"What can we do for you?" she said, taking Flint's coffee, turning the chair around and sitting down at the table. Flint went back to the counter to pour himself another cup.

"You know the guy they've got at the hospital--the one who lost his memory?"

"Yeah, what about him?"

"We want him back."

MacVean arched her eyebrows. "Meaning?"

"Meaning he ran away from Stoner and must have fallen down that gully in the dark. We can't come out and claim him, however, because the Health Department would get on our case for letting him escape in the first place."

MacVean nodded her head to show that she was following Gustafsson's logic.

"So, we need some help getting him back."

MacVean looked over at Flint who had just sat down. "What do you think about that?" she asked her boyfriend. "These people lose their patient and want us to bring him back home. How do you expect us do that?" she said turning back to Gustafsson. "Walk into the hospital and say excuse me, this man needs to go bye-bye?"

Gustafsson smiled to show MacVean that he appreciated her sense of humor. She was being a hard ass, but what else could you expect from a dirty cop?

"How long you think they'll keep him there?" Gustafsson asked Flint.

"Couple of months," Flint replied. "His leg's still in a cast and his arm is broke. He doesn't even know his own name. My guess is that he'll stay put 'til some higher-up decides what to do with him."

"We need you to keep us informed about his progress. We need to know if he starts remembering things or if they're about to move him. We need to know who visits him, what medications they're giving him, if he makes any phone calls. The works."

"That'll cost you," Flint said.

Gustafsson ignored the remark. What'd the guy think––they'd ask him to do stuff for free?

"Then what?" MacVean asked.

"Then if something further needs to be done, we'll talk about what, where and when."

"And how much," Flint butted in again.

MacVean raised her hand for her partner to stop talking. "It'll cost you a grand a week," she said.

Gustafsson nodded. He'd been prepared to pay more. "We want daily reports. You guys got a fax machine?"

"No, but we can get one," MacVean answered.

"Get one and fax us copies of any documents you can put your hands on...but don't get caught! If you do, we never had this meeting and I have no idea what you're talking about."

Flint's mouth hardened. "I won't get caught," he said. "I may just be a technician, but I know people in that hospital."

Gustafsson ignored him. "Here's five grand in cash," Gustafsson said taking an envelope out of his pocket and placing it in front of MacVean. "The fax number is written on the envelope--so's my phone number. I expect to hear from you every day. I'll be back when that runs out." He got up. MacVean stood also and offered him her hand again. Guess she thought that's what men did when they made deals--shook hands. Maybe in the movies Gustafsson thought as he backed out of the driveway.

On the drive back north he called Plentikov. "How'd it go?" the doctor asked.

"They're on board," Gustafsson replied.

"Good," Plentikov said. "Now we wait for the right moment to eliminate the problem."

Chapter Fifteen

(Thursday, January 19, 2006)

Mac Johnson, as the hospital officially referred to the still unidentified patient, was not allowed to walk from his room to the entrance of the hospital on his discharge day. "It's standard procedure," the discharge nurse informed him. At least Nurse Richardson was there to wheel him down the long corridor to the front entrance. Before he could be released, however, he had to sign numerous forms. He was told to use "Mac Johnson" as his signature as long as he truly could not remember his real name and was not trying to defraud the hospital or the government.

Medicaid approved his disability application a week before he was discharged, which also meant he would have a source of income until such time as he was physically able to take a job.

As the day when he would be able to leave the hospital came near, the Fulton County Department of Social Services agreed to help find him an apartment and supply him some clothing and other necessities. They had him apply for food stamps and he was given $200 in cash on the day he left the hospital to tide him over until his first Medicaid check arrived.

Mark Weathers, the caseworker assigned to Mac, was a forty-something year old whose standard wardrobe consisted of a faded green corduroy jacket, a blue buttoned-down shirt with frayed sleeves and brown corduroy pants. He'd visited Mac a few times in the hospital and promised to be at the hospital entrance on Mac's discharge day.

Denise Richardson had instructed Weathers to bring his car into the traffic circle by the hospital front entrance given that the outside temperature was twenty degrees with a wind chill factor that made it feel like zero. Although the front sidewalk had been shoveled, the icy surface made it difficult for Richardson to maneuver the wheelchair. Seeing her falter, Mac told her to stop. "I can manage from here," he said. He got up slowly, then almost fell.

The hospital physical therapy staff had worked with Mac in sessions that started even before the cast on his leg came off. Social Services provided a pair of shoes. But the soles of the first pair were worn on an angle and the physical therapy staff sent them back. A second pair came in better condition even though they were a half size too big. In addition to the shoes, Social Services supplied Mac with two pair of pants—one blue jeans and one pair of khakis, three shirts—one flannel with a red and green plaid pattern, one blue lined flannel shirt and one plain cotton white dress shirt along with several pair of socks and underwear.

Prior to each P.T. session, he was allowed to exchange his hospital gown for his street clothes although hospital regulation required that he be wheel-chaired to the P.T. room. There, in the course of a couple of weeks, he began to regain strength. The limp in his walk would slowly disappear they told him if he kept up the exercises they prescribed for him.

The cast on his wrist had come off two weeks prior to the leg cast and while he was learning to walk again, the P.T. staff had him go through a series of motion exercises for the wrist. At first, the range was limited and he experienced flashes of pain, but eventually the range of motion increased and it didn't hurt to put weight on his right hand when he pushed himself to a seated position on his hospital bed.

Mac faced leaving the hospital with mixed emotions. He wanted to manage on his own, but what kind of life would he have? Walking to Mark Weathers' car with the cold wind whistling around his head, he wondered if he was truly ready for the outside world.

"Your big day," Weathers said, when Mac got into the car.

"I'm a little nervous," Mac replied, as Weathers drove out of the traffic circle to the hospital exit lane.

Weathers took being assigned to this missing person as confirmation of his close relationship with Bertha Huckins, the executive director of the Fulton County Department of Social Services. Having hitched his wagon to Huckins' star when she was a controversial appointment of a controversial city mayor three and a half years ago, Weathers was often rewarded with such plums as first choice of holiday and vacations days and his choice of cases.

The case of the man who lost his memory was one that Weathers was happy to accept. Yes, it meant extra paperwork necessitated by having to report to the State Police, but it also meant that other case workers would catch some of the routine cases that would otherwise have been assigned to him. But the real reason he wanted the case was that people were still talking about the man who'd lost his memory. What would that be like Weathers wondered? Would he be able to function in the real world?

On one hand, Weathers wanted the client to know he was getting special treatment by being assigned to the agency's top caseworker, but on the other hand, he didn't want the guy to think he could have whatever he asked for. Early on he'd look for an opportunity to deny a request.

"Are you concerned that some day you'll wake up and not know where you are?" Weathers asked Mac while waiting for a traffic light.

"What do you mean?"

"If your memory came back all of a sudden, for example," Weathers said. "Maybe you wouldn't remember anything that happened after your accident."

Mac contemplated that scenario. During the weeks he lay in his hospital bed bored by the TV shows and the limited choices of reading matter available from the hospital library, he was unable to crystallize anything more than vague images of his past. In the end, he became reconciled with the need to establish a new life with a new identity.

Dr. Chassen, the hospital psychologist, told Mac that he might have trouble making decisions at first given how little he knew about himself. He suggested that Mac use his amnesia as an opportunity to become the kind of person he wanted to be. "You've no baggage to prevent you from becoming very different from your former self."

Nothing except the fact that he was past forty, was recovering from serious injuries and had no job and no money.

Dr. Bhatt told him he had not been in good health prior to the accident--although Bhatt did not share all of the details of the blood tests that resulted in his being given massive dosages of vitamins and minerals to prevent illness and to help his body recover from his injuries. As a result, Mac didn't understand why Dr. Chassen insisted that he meet with the hospital nutritionist. In their first meeting, using a tone that suggested it had been his fault for allowing his health to deteriorate, she informed him that he should eat fruits and vegetables daily and stay away from fatty foods and sugars. He tried to tell her that he knew all that, but she seemed intent on giving her spiel, so Mac listened and nodded at the appropriate moments.

He did discover a few things about himself in the sessions with the nutritionist. He realized that he knew quite a bit about cooking. When he remarked on that fact to Denise Richardson, she suggested that meant that he might have been a bachelor, on the assumption that had he been married, his wife would probably have done the cooking.

Mac didn't think that was the case, however. It was just a feeling he had, but when he thought about whether he'd been married or single, married felt right. He wasn't sure if he should convey that fact to Richardson, however, since she wasn't wearing a wedding ring. Maybe she was married, but took her ring off at work? He tried to work up the courage to ask

Richardson about her private life, but never found the right time. She was always pleasant, but professional. Mac decided not to press her since he counted on her cheerful smile to keep himself from despairing over his likely future.

"Dr. Bhatt said I might begin to remember things little by little," Mac told Weathers.

"Here we are," Weathers said pulling into the driveway next to a large yellow two-story house.

Mac considered his new home and the neighborhood in which it was situated. The building looked neglected. It needed a paint job and probably new windows all around. The houses on each side were in similar condition.

"Bring your bag," Weathers instructed getting out of the car. Mac walked gingerly. The sidewalk had only been cleared a single shovel's width. The thin jacket Weathers had brought Mac earlier that week provided little resistance against the cold wind that blew across the front yard. Weathers wore a pair of black leather gloves but had failed to provide Mac with either gloves or boots.

Mac stood shivering on the steps. All of his worldly belongings fit into one brown grocery bag. He wanted to ask why he wasn't given warmer clothing, but he knew he ought to be grateful that Social Services had found him a place to live.

Weathers was having trouble opening the outside door. He tried several of the keys that hung on a ring of keys before discovering that the outside door was unlocked.

Inside the front door was a small hall with a stairway to the second floor and a door to the right. Weathers told Mac they had found him a first floor apartment because of the difficulty he might have climbing stairs due to his injuries. It took Weathers a minute to find the key to the inside door. The door opened into a small living room with a bricked-in fireplace. The furniture consisted of a scratched up coffee table with an old issue of Time Magazine on it and a saggy couch with a grayish corduroy cover and a matching easy chair.

Weathers led Mac through the front room into a fairly large kitchen. Other than a refrigerator and a stove, the furniture in the room consisted of a table with metal legs, a Formica top and four non-matching chairs.

"This is the kitchen," Weathers said after he turned on the overhead light.

Mac nodded. It was not warm enough in the house to prevent a layer of frost from covering the kitchen windows. Wiping his hand on a back wall window, he was able to see a snow-covered back yard. "Where's the bedroom?" he asked.

Weathers walked towards a door off the kitchen. Inside was a small dark room with a bed, a chest of drawers and a bedside table. The sole window on the far wall had a shade, but no curtain. Mac flipped the switch on the wall, which turned on an overhead light housed in a fixture whose glass cover had not been cleaned recently, if ever.

"There should be a set of sheets and a blanket in the bottom drawer," Weathers said.

Mac opened the drawer and took out a single set of sheets and a thin grey army blanket. "No pillow?" he inquired.

"No?" Weathers said. "You can get one at Wal-Mart. Let's see what else you need."

They examined the kitchen cupboards discovering an unmatched set of dishes, some silverware, a saucepan and a scratched up 10-inch formerly Teflon-coated frying pan.

"This isn't really safe to cook with," Mac said pointing to the pan.

"Wal-Mart," Weathers replied.

"How do I get there?"

"It's not far. You can catch a bus. Make a list of what you need and I'll see what we can do," Weathers said, looking at his watch. It was close to lunch time.

Mac looked around for paper and a pencil. He found a few scraps of paper in a drawer with a ballpoint pen, but the pen didn't write. "Can I borrow your pen?"

Weathers had two pens in his shirt pocket––a gold-plated Cross pen and a Bic.

"Keep it," he told Mac, giving him the Bic.

Mac started to make up a list of things he thought he might need. "Did you say you're taking me to the Wal-Mart?"

Weathers looked at his watch. "I really don't have a lot of time," Weathers said. If he took the guy, he could tell Huckins. She'd appreciate the fact that he went the extra mile.

"Don't worry about it then," Mac said.

Weathers grimaced. "No, it's all right. Make up your list and I'll take you."

Chapter Sixteen

(Same Day)

An hour and a half later, Weathers left Mac on his own.

Weathers had explained that the landlord controlled the thermostat. Supposedly he'd been there earlier that morning to move it up to 68. A lock had been placed on the unit preventing anyone from changing the setting. In the time they'd been at the Wal-Mart and the neighboring supermarket, the apartment had not warmed up sufficiently for Mac to take off his thin jacket.

He put away the groceries he'd purchased with the food stamp card. Thank goodness Weathers had gone with him because he would have used up most of his cash on items not covered by the food stamp program. Weathers charged Social Services for a pillow and two pillowcases, a second blanket and some additional clothes including a hooded sweatshirt, a pair of rubber boots and a pair of gloves.

Mac decided to make the bed. He sat down on it when he'd finished. The mattress must be twenty years old. He got up and put away his clothes.

The bedroom was colder than the kitchen. He barely felt any warmth coming out of the heating vent. He left the bedroom door open to try to warm it up.

He was hungry. He'd purchased several cans of soup, a large jar of peanut butter, and a jar of strawberry jam as well as frozen dinners.

The kitchen contained neither a microwave oven nor a toaster.

"Why bother?" he said out loud.

Why not close all the doors and turn on the gas stove? He got out of his chair and walked over to the stove. *Why not?* No one would miss him.

Well, maybe Denise Richardson would shed a tear, but she had plenty of other patients to worry about.

If he had tried to commit suicide by throwing himself into that gully, why not finish the job? As things stood, he was just a burden on society.

But, whenever he thought about the possibility that he'd tried to take his own life, he wasn't convinced. It didn't feel right. First, throwing oneself down a gully was not the most logical way to do oneself in. Plus, how did he get there in the first place?

No, the most likely explanation was that someone took him there and threw him down the gully expecting him to perish. Either that or he fell accidentally. But what undermined the latter scenario was the lack of a vehicle that would explain how he'd come to that location. Since there was no village within fifteen miles, it was very unlikely he'd walked there. Plus, the clothes he was wearing when they found him were not those one would wear for a hike in the middle of October in the Adirondacks where the nights that time of year were often below freezing.

If someone had tried to kill him, shouldn't he try to find out who it was? Didn't he want to know why they wanted him dead? Shouldn't he try to help the State Police catch the culprit? He couldn't imagine at the moment how he'd do that, but what if he could?

Mac found a can opener and a saucepan. He opened a can of tomato soup and poured the contents into the pan, added some water and put it on the stove.

Right now his only reason to live was to gain a measure of revenge against those who wanted him dead. But in order to survive, he needed a plan. One thing he had in his favor was that his enemies might not know that he'd survived. If they thought he was dead, he might be okay. But what if they found out? They'd surely try to find him with the goal of finishing him off.

He needed to be ready to defend himself in case they showed up on his doorstep, and he needed to find something to do with his time.

Sitting down with a piece of paper, Mac made some notes while he ate. An hour later he had a list of things he wanted to try to do over the next week or two.

He was extremely vulnerable. It would be very easy for someone who wanted to kill him to do so. Once he'd decided to live, he made a vow: he wasn't going down without a fight. The problem was he wasn't sure how much of a fight he could put up.

Peter G. Pollak

Chapter Seventeen

(Saturday, January 21, 2006)

"Can't you sit still for a whole minute?" Thom Flowers demanded of Bernard Floer.

Bernard, who had just gotten out of his leather La-Z-Boy, stopped in the middle of the room. "I was only going to poke the fire. It looked like it was going to die out."

"That's the third time you've 'poked' that poor fire," Thom replied. "And, the third time you asked me if I'd like another Kahlua and the third time you checked to see if the back door was locked, and I don't know what else, except sit and read your book."

"You exaggerate," Bernard said. "I only went to check on the back door once."

Thom put his book down on the coffee table next to his empty liqueur glass. "I thought you were looking forward to a quiet evening at home reading."

"I was and I am," Bernard replied.

"How many pages have you read?" Thom demanded.

"Who's keeping count?"

"I'll bet you haven't read ten pages since we got home."

"That book isn't grabbing me," Bernard confessed. "Maybe I'll try something else."

Thom shook his head. "It's not the book.

Something's on your mind and I wish you'd deal with it before you drive me to my bed."

"Well," Bernard said. "So much for 'romance in the old manse.'"

Thom ignored the phrase that he'd uttered on their first night together in the farmhouse they'd purchased and remodeled a decade before. "How romantic do you think it is watching you wrestling with something when you won't even tell me what it is?"

"You know what it is," Bernard replied. "I told you over dinner."

Thom got up and walked over to the liqueur cabinet. He uncorked a bottle of Kahlua and filled his glass. They had eaten a leisurely dinner in their favorite restaurant, the George Mann Tory Tavern, braving the January cold for the satisfaction of old French wines and a well-cooked meal.

"We discussed many things," Thom said after he sat back down on the couch, "--how your project is coming, your plans for next month's photo shoot in Quebec, how much you hate waiting in line at the bank in town while the teller and customer discuss crop yields."

"And…"

"And what?"

"And that I'm worried about the man I rescued."

Thom sipped down his drink. "So that's what's got your jock strap in an uproar."

"It has nothing to do with any jock strap, which is not an item I possess by the way," Floer said. "I just need to make sure he's doing okay."

"So, what's stopping you? Not me, for God's sake."

Floer grimaced. He was the jealous one in their relationship. They'd met at a welcoming party for Flowers who'd just been named director of the Old Stone Fort Museum. Floer had been hired to photograph the event. They had got to talking as Floer followed him around, taking his pictures and helping Flowers identify people whose names he needed to remember and those he didn't.

Bernard quickly figured out that Flowers was gay. "You know if Flowers and Floer got married neither would have to change their last name," he joked at the end of the evening.

Flowers turned bright red. It was a good minute before he said anything. "I didn't realize my gender preference was so obvious."

"I figured it out when you avoided starring at Mrs. Forest's cleavage," Bernard said.

Thom smiled. "She certainly flaunts it, doesn't she?"

Bernard nodded. "Not to worry. I won't tell a soul."

"How are things up here in the sticks for us gays?" Thom asked.

"There are a couple of taverns you definitely want to stay out of," Bernard replied. "And, if you bring your boyfriend up here from the city, don't walk down Main Street holding hands."

A year later they decided to purchase a house and move in together.

Bernard sat back in his chair. "I guess I'll drive up there. The hospital gave me an address, but they didn't have a phone number."

"You tried calling information?"

"I'm not sure what name he's using. Remember, he can't recall his real name."

"Oh, right."

Bernard started to get up, but then realized what he was doing and sat back. "It's funny. I read someplace that if you save someone's life, you become attached to them permanently."

Thom arched his eyebrows. "Oh?"

"You know what I mean," Bernard said. "Plus, I got to thinking about how he got in that gully in the first place. If someone meant to kill him, won't they try again?"

"I suppose…if they know he's alive and where he's living."

"That's why I've got to see him--to make sure he understands he could be in danger."

"As I said, no one's stopping you."

Bernard sighed. "You're right. I'll be back from New York late Wednesday. I'm free Thursday. I'll go then."

Chapter Eighteen

(Monday, January 23, 2006)

Mac screwed up his courage and knocked on the door. No answer. He knocked again. "Who's there?" came the response. Sounded like the man of the house, or apartment as it were.

"Your new neighbor," Mac replied.

"What do you want?"

Nothing. Never mind. Sorry to have bothered you. "I just wanted to introduce myself."

"Just a minute then."

Probably had to put on some clothes, although if the temperature on the second floor was anything like that in his apartment, the man was unlikely to be running around naked.

Mac thought about what he wanted to say while waiting. Part of his plan to protect himself was to get to know his neighbors and enlist them in watching out for each other. Would they buy it?

The door opened half way. The man blocking the doorway looked to be in his late forties––balding, beer-belly gut protruding from his Hofner's Laundry uniform shirt. His reading glasses protruded from his shirt pocket. *A baseball bat behind his back?*

"I'm sorry if I caught you at a bad time," Mac began.

"I just got home," the man said.

"My name is Mac. Mac Johnson." Mac stuck out his hand. The man ignored it. "I just moved in downstairs. Thought I ought to let you know so you wouldn't call the cops on me."

The man kept a firm grip on the door. "We mind our own business."

Mac withdrew his hand. *I get it. You wish I'd done so too.* "I don't blame you. I did have a couple things I was going to ask the landlord to do--you know, to make the place a little safer. I thought maybe we'd work as a team."

"He's not gonna fix anything that the law don't say he's got to fix."

"I'll bet replacing a burned out bulb on the front porch qualifies," Mac suggested.

The man shrugged.

"And, I really think there ought to be a light in the back."

The man shook his head. "Our bedroom's in the back."

"They have the kind that operate on motion. You know motion detectors. Wouldn't be on all the time."

"You can ask him, but he won't do it."

The man still hadn't told Mac his name. Of course, Mac had checked the mailbox when adding his own name, but all it said was 'upstairs.'

"We'll, again I'm sorry to have bothered you Mr.--"

The man hesitated. "Kohler."

"Mr. Kohler. Oh, and one more thing. Who's responsible for shovelling the walk?"

"The landlord."

"I assume he hires someone to do it?"

"Kid from down the street."

"He really could do a better job don't you think?"

Kohler shrugged.

"I figure the more things I bring up, the greater the likelihood that the landlord will do something. You know what I mean?"

Kohler didn't even bother to shrug in answer to that comment. He turned as if listening to someone in a back room. "My dinner's ready."

"Well then. Nice to meet you."

Mac turned and walked cautiously down the wooden steps. Back in his apartment, he went over to the kitchen table and sat down. He rubbed his face. *No help there.* He still could try the people who lived in the houses on either side of his, but they'd probably give him the same kind of reception.

Having decided he wanted to live, Mac spent his first full day on his own going over the items on his list of things he wanted to do to make it hard for his unknown enemies to finish him off.

His first floor apartment was vulnerable in almost every conceivable way. The back door was solid, but with the settling of the house, the latch mechanism didn't line up with the strike plate cleanly. A good blow could knock it open. He would ask the landlord for a dead-bolt lock, but compounding the vulnerability of the back door was the fact that there were no lights in the back of the house.

He couldn't come out and tell any of his neighbors that someone might try to kill him. He'd have to be subtle, suggest that they watch out for each other. Given the number of house burglaries that he'd read about in the newspaper, he thought he could be convincing on that point. He'd ask them to report to each other any strangers they saw hanging out in the neighborhood to guard against people casing their houses.

What about a weapon? He knew he wouldn't qualify to purchase a gun--given that he didn't know his real name and history. He could purchase a couple of baseball bats, which he could leave strategically around the apartment. That thought made him laugh. Anyone who wanted him dead would be armed to the teeth.

The bottom line was whatever he thought might help would cost money and, since the amount he would be getting from Medicaid would barely cover his food, rent and utilities, he needed to find a job.

The Help Wanted section in the Gloversville *Leader Herald*, which he purchased from the corner grocery, wasn't particularly helpful. There were only two items he thought he might qualify for, but when he called, one of the positions had been filled and the other required transportation, which of course he didn't have.

Mark Weathers had suggested he visit the employment office on Main Street at the opposite end of town. Figuring there was no time like the present Mac set out right after breakfast day two.

The receptionist at the employment office gave Mac several forms to fill out. He filled in his name--Mac Johnson and his address, but the next blank asked for date of birth. No clue. Next blank: social security number? He didn't have one. Education? He'd have to leave that blank. Work history? Same. References? Who could he put down? Answer: no one.

He looked through the rest of the form, but there was nothing else he could fill in. Who was going to hire someone with just a name and address--and a temporary, made-up name at that?

He thought of leaving, but reluctantly turned in the form.

Mac heard someone call his name. A man holding his application form was looking around the room over the top of his glasses. He was short, thin and balding. Mac followed him into a cubicle. His name badge identified him as Jonathan Corwin, Employment Counselor.

"Mr. Johnson," he stated, motioning for Mac to take a seat. "You say you want a job involving bookkeeping or accounting, but you offer no evidence of your competence in those fields. You didn't even fill out the minimum information that the form asks for starting with your social security number and your date of birth. How do you expect us to help you if you're not willing to provide that essential information? No business is going to trust its books to a man who isn't qualified."

Mac didn't have an answer.

"Further, Mr. Johnson. Is that how someone dresses who is applying for a professional profession? Are you aware that professionals still wear suits and ties to work these days? It's extremely unlikely that we can place you in one of those categories, but I'll do my best to find something that's more appropriate to your educational background and skill set. So, I'm going to give this application back to you and you can either fill it out properly or, if you're unwilling to do so, I'm afraid we can't help you."

Mac felt himself shriveling down in the chair as the counselor made his little speech.

"Well, which will it be?" Corwin asked when Mac didn't respond immediately.

"Mr. Corwin," Mac began. "It's not that I didn't want to fill out that information. I was in a bad accident six months ago. I can't remember where I went to school or what my last job was or even my date of birth. I've applied for a new social security number, but it hasn't come yet. I just know that I need a job."

Corwin didn't look like that explanation satisfied him. "And can you prove any of that?"

Mac retrieved Mark Weathers' business card from his shirt pocket. "Call this gentleman at the Fulton County Department of Social Services. He'll verify what I've told you."

Mr. Corwin took the card. "Fine. Call here two days from now between the hours of ten and noon and ask for me. I'll let you know if there's anything open."

With that, Mac had to go back outside into the cold winter air. A schedule posted at the bus stop said the next bus heading north on Main Street wouldn't be there for 30 minutes. He started walking.

Chapter Nineteen

(Tuesday, January 24, 2006)

Denise Richardson turned off her TV. What would be the harm, she asked herself? She put on her boots and coat and headed out to her car.

She drove up East Fulton St. to Route 29 and turned left towards the Wal-Mart. Denise had decided to buy Mac Johnson a house-warming present. That was as good an excuse to stop by to see him as anything else.

She wasn't sure what her interest in him was. Yes, she felt sorry for him. Waking up with no memory of your past--not even your name! She couldn't imagine. But was that all?

She remembered Mac telling the man from the state police that he thought he had children. Two girls, didn't he say? That probably meant there was a woman someplace wondering what happened to her husband.

Denise worried that she should keep her distance. Divorced and childless she had tumbled into too many bad relationships since her husband ran off the with Laborers' Union treasury. But Mac Johnson didn't know anyone in Gloversville. Everyone needed at least one friend.

Forty-five minutes later, she knocked on his apartment door, holding a gift-wrapped package. No answer at first. She was about to leave, when the door opened. It was Mac.

"I thought I heard someone knocking."

"That was me," Denise said. "I tried the doorbell first."

"It doesn't work. It's on my list of things I'd like the landlord to fix."

"Here," she said, handing him the package.

"What's this?"

"A house-warming gift."

"Wow. That's very kind, but you didn't have to."

She smiled. "Of course I didn't."

"Come in. Come in," Mac said. "I'm sorry for being so rude, making you stand out here in the cold."

"Just for a minute. I've got to be at work at three."

He led her into the apartment.

"Can I offer you a cup of coffee or tea? In teas, I've got decaf green or regular."

"That's not necessary."

"It's no trouble really."

"Well, okay. I'll have tea. Regular please."

"Coming right up." He put on the kettle and got out two mugs. "If I'd known you were coming I'd have bought some cookies," he said with a wink.

She chuckled. She studied him as he got two mugs out of the cupboard. He still limped pretty badly, but seemed to be moving better. He had kept the beard, but it was neat. She liked it on him.

He pulled out a chair from the kitchen table for her and sat down on the opposite side.

"How are things at the hospital?"

"Oh, the same."

"Any more strangers show up with no memory?"

She liked that he was trying to be humorous. "No, you're the only one we've had lately."

His face got serious. "Thank goodness. I wouldn't wish that on my worst enemy."

"I understand. That's part of the reason I wanted to stop by to see how you are making out."

"Great," he said, then paused. "Yeah, everything's great."

She gave him a hard look. "You can be honest with me, Mac. I'm not here to judge you."

"Thank you," he replied. "Thank you, Nurse Richardson. I appreciate that."

"Denise, please. You're no longer my patient."

"Okay, Denise. To be honest, things are not all that great. I'm living here in this not so attractive apartment with no job, no money, no family, no friends--"

"Stop right there," Denise said putting her hand on top of his. "You've got one friend."

He looked away from her. She thought he was going to cry. "Thank you Nurse...Denise. Thank you. You don't know how much that means to me."

"And, Gloversville's not such a bad place once you get to know it. There are lots of decent people living here. Give it time."

He nodded. The teakettle started to whistle. He poured the hot water over two tea bags and brought the mugs to the table.

"Open your present," Denise said.

"Okay. This is so nice of you." He took off the wrapping paper carefully rather than tearing it off like a kid would do. It was a set of kitchen towels, potholders and dishrags.

"I thought you might need these," she said.

"I do. The stuff that came with this apartment is older than sin--if you know what I mean."

"I'm glad you like it." She looked at her watch. "Oops. It's time for me to get going."

She stood up. He got up with her.

"Do you have a phone, Mac?"

"Not yet. One is on order."

"When you get it installed, please call me. Here's my number." She gave him a slip of paper with her phone number.

"I will," he said. "Thank you, Denise. I can't--"

"The best way to thank me, Mac, is by not giving up. Maybe some day your memory will come back and you'll be reunited with your family. Meanwhile, take it day by day. That's all anyone can ask of you."

She thought about giving him a hug, but worried about how he'd interpret it. She worried about her own motivation as well. Was it maternal instinct or loneliness crying out for human contact?

Chapter Twenty

(Same Day)

Mac started to unwrap the towel set, but sat down and put his head in his hands. He was on the verge of crying. He didn't know why Denise's visit had upset him so, but he felt lonelier at that moment than he had before her visit. You don't know how lonely you can be, he thought to himself, until your only friend in the world has left.

After a few minutes, he roused himself from his chair and went to wash the mugs. He decided he would allow himself fifteen minutes to work on that day's crossword puzzle from the newspaper. The crossword and other puzzles in the paper were one of the few things he had to look forward to each day.

He was lost in the puzzle when he heard a knock on his door. Maybe Denise had come back for some reason. He looked around thinking she might have left something. That didn't seem to be the case.

The knocking was repeated. Mac went to the door. It was Mark Weathers.

"Glad I found you home," Weathers said, pushing himself into the front room. "Get your coat. We're going down to the Employment Office."

Mac got his coat and followed Weathers to his car. "What's up?" he asked as Weathers pulled away from the curb.

"You had a meeting with a Jonathan Corwin yesterday, right?"

Mac nodded. *Oh, oh. What could this be about?*

"He called me today and, after I straightened him out, he said he may have something for you."

Mac sighed. "That would be great."

"I'll admit I was skeptical when we met the other day," Jonathan Corwin said to Mac after the three of them were seated in an Employment Office interview cubicle. "But, Mr. Weathers explained your circumstances. That said, your opportunities are still extremely limited, as most anyone who is looking for a bookkeeper or an accountant needs to know the person they hire not only has credentials and job history, but is honest and has good references. However, there is one situation that may just work out."

"What's that?" Mark Weathers asked.

"There's a company in Johnstown--Foster Industries. I'm sure you've heard of it," he said to Weathers. He faced Mac. "They manufacture replacement windows and doors and they are looking for someone for twenty hours a week with bookkeeping experience to assist their regular bookkeeper. I know the president of the company. We've helped them find people in the past. I think he can be persuaded to give you a chance."

"Excellent," Weathers said.

Mac nodded.

"It's not a done deal yet. One thing in your client's favor is that we have no one else to send. Also, as a part-time assistant, the burden of responsibility for accuracy and so forth would still remain on the shoulders of their fulltime person. But, I'm sure Eliot Anderson is not going to accept you on some vague supposition that you know what you're doing. He'll want us to test you to find out whether you know bookkeeping basics and can perform the necessary tasks for the job."

"That sounds fair," Weathers said, looking at Mac for confirmation. Mac nodded.

"What do you have in mind?" Mac asked.

"We'll set up a test. It'll take me a few days to get the test materials. I'll get working on it and give you a call when everything is in place."

Weathers turned to Mac. "Does that sound okay to you?"

Mac nodded. "It sounds more than fair. I'll give it a try."

"Good," Corwin said. "Expect to hear from me in a few days."

Mac thought about having to take a bookkeeping test on the ride home. Would he come up blank just like he did when trying to remember his past?

Weathers pulled into the driveway when he reached Mac's building. "I can't come in, but I wanted to ask you how you're doing?"

"It's not been easy," Mac admitted, "but having a job––even a part-time one––should help."

"There is the issue of your getting back and forth to the job," Weathers pointed out.

"I hadn't thought about that," Mac confessed.

"You'll have to take the bus. I left you the Gloversville Transit Authority schedule the other day, right?"

Mac nodded.

"I believe they service the Johnstown Industrial Park where Foster is located. Check the schedule. Then when you talk to them about your hours you will be able to tell them what time you can get there."

"What about studying for the test?" Mac asked.

"Good thought," Weathers replied. "Try the public library. They may have some books you can use. Anything else?"

"Yes. I've tried to contact the landlord about some problems with the apartment."

"Like what?"

"The back door for example. It has a lock but anyone could bust through it easily enough. I asked them to install a dead-bolt lock on the inside. His secretary said they'd consider it."

"That sounds reasonable," Weathers said.

"There's also the matter of replacing the burned-out bulbs on the front porch. When I moved in, one bulb was out; now a second one's gone."

"They should take care of that. You're absolutely right."

"I wonder if they'd move faster if you contacted them," Mac suggested.

Weathers thought for a minute. "Give them another week. If they haven't done anything or gotten back to you, I'll give them a call."

"A week? To tell the truth, Mr. Weathers, I don't feel safe there."

"No? I'll admit there is a bit of a crime problem in Gloversville, but I don't think you need to worry. The people who are doing the breaking and entering stick to the high end neighborhoods."

"I'm not worried about thieves," Mac confessed. "Someone tried to kill me, Mr. Weathers. What if they find out I'm still alive?"

Weathers thought for a second. "Okay. I get your point. I'll call your landlord first thing in the morning.

How's that?"

Mac entered his apartment. Things were going as well as could be expected. There was a good chance he'd have a job in a week or two and five days had gone by and there was no sign of whoever had tried to kill him.

On the other hand, if they were out there, it was only a matter of time. He hoped Mr. Weathers would be true to his word. If not, he had no idea where to turn.

Peter G. Pollak

Chapter Twenty-One

(Thursday, January 26, 2006)

By midday the following day, the constant worrying about how and when he might be attacked was taking its toll. Mac paced his kitchen floor, trying to decide whether to remain in the apartment or go someplace else, despite the fact that it was snowing heavily outside and the wind chill was reported to be in the teens.

He wanted to leave. The only place he could think of where he could hang out for a few hours was the public library. But then he'd have to come home and it would be dark and he'd be back where he started--except it would be night. Nights were worse than days--much worse.

As the sky darkened each afternoon, Mac felt his blood pressure rising. He became anxious and went around the house turning on all of the lights.

Night was when he'd be most vulnerable to an attack. He wouldn't sleep in the bedroom because he assumed that's where any assailants would expect to find him.

Instead, each night he stuffed some pillows under the blankets on the bed to make it look like a body, then tried to make himself comfortable on the living room couch. But he slept fitfully, even with that ruse, waking at any small noise--whether it was the refrigerator compressor starting up or turning off or the sound of one of the people overhead flushing the toilet or the wind banging a loose shutter. Once awake, he'd sit there in the dark, listening for the sound that would confirm his worse fears––that they'd found him and he was as sure as dead. Only towards morning would sleep overtake him, but he never woke up refreshed.

Despite the weather outside, Mac decided a few hours at the library with other people around would give him some respite. He was in the front hall putting on his boots, when someone knocked on his front door.

His first instinct was to remain perfectly still and hope whomever it was would go away. Then, he realized it might be Denise Richardson.

Opening the door with the safety chain in place, he saw the back of a man whom he didn't recognize … until the man turned around so that Mac could see his face. It was Bernard Floer, the photographer who had saved his life.

"Just a minute." He freed the safety chain, then opened the door. "Hello, Mr. Floer, this is a surprise."

"Call me Bernard, please."

"Bernard. Nice to see you."

"I'm sorry to drop in on you this way," Bernard said, "but the people at the hospital didn't know if you had a phone. I practically had to file a law suit to get them to give out your street address."

"I'm glad they did," Mac said. "Come on in."

"You have your boots on," Bernard Floer said. "Were you coming in or on your way out?"

"Out. I was just going down to the library."

"In this weather? I hope you have a car?"

"No, I don't. I was going to try to catch the bus. I guess it's pretty nasty out there?"

"It sure is. If I'd have known it was going to be this bad, I would have waited and come up another day."

Mac ushered Floer into his kitchen. "I'm glad you decided to visit. Can I make you some tea or coffee?"

"That'd be nice. Then, if you still want to go to the library, I'll give you a ride."

Fifteen minutes, a cup of tea and some small talk later, Bernard got around to the reason for his visit. "I've been thinking a lot about your situation," he began. "There has to be a logical explanation as to how you ended up in that desolate location. Have you remembered anything more since we last talked?"

Mac shook his head. "I've tried all kinds of tricks to jar my memory, but nothing seems to help."

"I can't imagine how that must feel," Bernard said.

"Some days it bothers me more than others." He didn't say today had been the worst with the weather raging around the house cutting down visibility. He felt like an animal trapped in a cage.

"As I said, I've been doing a lot of thinking about what happened to you," Floer continued. "Given that you had no identification on your person and that the State Police didn't find an abandoned vehicle nearby that they could trace to you, it seems to me there are only two possibilities--either someone drove you there or you walked."

"Okay," Mac said. "That makes sense."

"I've studied the maps of the region. The nearest village is Meadow Lake, which is about fifteen miles north of where you were found. Fifteen miles is a long, but not impossible walk, but if you walked from Meadow Lake, you would have had to have left your car there and eventually someone would have noticed an abandoned car and that would have enabled the State Police to discover your identity."

"Wow, you really have been giving this some thought."

"I have. It's funny, but after saving your life, I kind of felt an obligation to do more, to help you find out how you got in that predicament--especially after I visited you at the hospital and you told me you'd lost your memory."

Mac took a sip of his tea. "You've already done so much, Bernard. I don't know how I'll ever thank you."

"No thanks necessary. If I can help you in any way, that'll be thanks enough."

"Well, if you wouldn't mind dropping me off at the library--"

"I'd be glad to do so, but let me try out one more thought," Floer said. "Tell me if you think I'm on the right track."

"Sure."

"Let's assume someone drove you to that location. So, here's an important question--did your doctors ever mention to you how long you'd been down in that gully?"

"Let me think a minute," Mac said. He got up and walked around the kitchen for a few seconds. "I do recall Dr. Bhatt saying that if you had not discovered me when you did, I'd probably have died of exposure before the end of the day."

"That doesn't help us. Okay. Let's assume you were driven there at night. Why? Even though Route 62 is a remote highway, no one would take the chance of parking their car by the side of the road in broad daylight, dragging you out of the car--assuming you were already unconscious or perhaps tied up--and then pushing you over the side. They'd do it at night, and probably after midnight when chances of someone coming along and seeing what was going on would be almost nil."

Mac nodded. "That sounds logical."

"So, why would they pick that location? Have you asked yourself that question?"

Mac shook his head. "Everyone says it's very remote."

"That it is. In fact, I learned that the locals call it 'Desolation Ridge,'" Floer replied, "but it's not the only remote location in the Adirondacks. In fact, there are probably dozens of equally remote locations where a person could be pushed off the road into a lake or a swamp or a rock-filled gully. Why that location?"

"Convenience, I suppose."

"Exactly. If I were going to dispose of someone, I would travel some distance from where I lived, but I wouldn't necessarily drive all night to find a location if I knew of one an hour or two away."

"Again, that makes sense to me."

"When I looked at a map of that region, I only found a handful of places that are two hours driving distance from where I found you, including several motels and hotels."

Mac's stomach took a tumble. Floer was making a lot of sense, but did he really want to know the truth? What it might reveal could be worse than not knowing.

"I called all of the hotels and motels and asked them if someone left a car in their parking lot, but none of them did. Then there are summer camps and religious retreats, but all of those close by Columbus Day. The only year-round facility within that distance is a mental health rehabilitation facility called Stoner Sanitarium. Does that name ring any bells?"

Mac shook his head. He didn't think he'd heard it, but then all of a sudden he remembered something. He'd seen the name Stoner before. An image floated just out of reach.

"Are you remembering something?" Bernard asked.

"Possibly," Mac replied. "I'm not sure, but I started to remember seeing that name on something. I just can't retrieve it. It's so frustrating."

"Perhaps you'd come across it in your profession," Bernard suggested. "The Sanitarium part is leftover from the days when they served tuberculosis patients. Today, apparently they serve primarily mentally ill patients, most of them private as opposed to paid for by the government."

Mac shook his head. "I just wish I could start to remember things."

"Don't feel bad. The fact that the name is not entirely foreign to you may be helpful. I'm going to contact Lieutenant Sheridan at the State Police and suggest he contact this facility."

"Again, you've done so much for me," Mac said.

Bernard stood up. "I haven't done enough if I can possibly help you further and don't do it. Now, let's get you over to the library."

Chapter Twenty-Two

(11:00 A.M., Monday, January 30, 2006)

Monday morning Mac had an appointment with Dr. Bhatt at the hospital for a routine check-up. The streets had finally been plowed and the sidewalks cleared from the previous week's snowstorm. He could not remember ever seeing such tall snow banks. The sky was a bright blue and the temperature was in the teens. Mac almost felt normal.

He'd only been home from the hospital a short time when he heard someone knocking at his front door.

Now who could it be? He felt less nervous about receiving visitors than he had the previous week. He opened the door with the chain latch.

A woman whom he did not recognize stood in the hallway.

"You wanted to know if anything strange was going on in the neighborhood, right?"

Because she wasn't wearing a coat, Mac realized she must be from upstairs. *Kohler was his name—is it hers?* "Hold on, I'll open the door."

"You wanted to know, right?

Mac nodded. "Did you see something suspicious?"

"There are these kids who've been walking by the house. I think they're casing it out."

"Really. What time of day?"

"Afternoon. About 3:30, 4:00."

Mac thought for a moment. "What do they look like?"

"Scruffy. They smoke cigarettes and they're always laughing and stuff."

"How old do you think they are?"

"Teenagers. Seventeen or older."

"Okay. Thanks for letting me know. Mrs. Kohler is it?"

She nodded. Mac wondered if she seriously thought a couple of teenagers represented a danger or if she had some other purpose in knocking on his door when her husband wasn't home. *Probably not.* She wore a flowery patterned dress that had seen better days, had stringy grayish blond hair and did strange things with her mouth as if her teeth hurt. "I'll watch for them this afternoon."

"I'm just trying to help."

"I appreciate it," Mac said. "We need to look out for each other."

She gave him a sad smile and turned and started up the stairs. "Oh. I almost forgot. I wanted to apologize for the other night."

"For what?" Mac asked.

"We woke you up, didn't we?"

In fact, they had. Saturday night or actually Sunday morning about two A.M., the Kohlers had stumbled in clearly drunk...stomping up the stairs and doing lots of yelling. Well, Mr. Kohler had done the yelling. Mac didn't recall her doing any yelling back.

"I'm a sound sleeper," Mac lied.

"It's the same every Saturday night. Mr. K and I go to the Step Out Inn for dinner and he promises not to have too many beers. But, after dinner, he wants to have one more at the bar and one more becomes six more and I have to drive home."

"Mrs. Kohler, you don't have to apologize to me."

"Well, I just wanted you to know. Every Saturday...even when the weather's shitty. He has to have his Saturday night out."

Mac waited until she disappeared before closing the door. He wasn't worried about a couple of teenagers, but Mrs. Kohler's visit did remind him that he hadn't talked to all of the neighbors on either side of his house. There was one more person he needed to call on.

Arthur Meyers lived on the top floor of the house next to Mac's building. He invited Mac in right away without asking him the purpose of his visit, offered him a cup of tea and once they were seated at his kitchen table started to tell his life history. He was 89 and had been born in 1917 in Stuttgart Germany. Fortunately, his father, who was in the leather business, saw what was coming and moved his family to the United States. "If he'd waited another year, they wouldn't have let us go," Meyers said.

His father started a leather export business in Gloversville. At its height, several family members including Arthur worked in the export business. "We did pretty well for a number of years, but when the glove industry started moving offshore, there wasn't enough business locally to continue."

"My father had passed on by then and I had to close it down. But I was fortunate. I found work with one of our competitors. I traveled all over the world, buying leather and selling finished goods."

"That must have been fascinating," Mac said.

"It was. Now I'm too old to travel, except in my mind," Meyer said with a chuckle.

Another lonely person Mac concluded. The visit

turned out to be a useful one, however. Meyers spent much of his day reading. His favorite spot was a big easy chair in the front room where he could observe the world go by.

"I did notice something strange the other day," Meyers said after Mac had explained the reason for his visit.

"What was that?"

"A man sitting in a car across the street. He was there for more than an hour. Then, when you went someplace with Mr. Weathers from Social Services, he left."

"So you know Mr. Weathers?" Mac inquired.

Mr. Meyers nodded. "He helped me get on food stamps."

"And you say the car followed us?"

"He left a few seconds after you pulled away, but I don't know how far he might have followed you."

Mac puzzled over the information.

Meyers, who walked with a cane, motioned for Mac to follow him to the front room. "He was parked over there," he said pointing to a spot under a large tree across the street. "I thought it was unusual for someone to sit that long in their car in this cold weather. He had the driver's side window open--I guess so the windows wouldn't fog up. That's how I know he never got out of that car."

"He was looking at my house?"

"Yes. He kept looking at it the whole time."

"What kind of car was it?"

"A Mercedes. I don't recall ever having seen a Mercedes parked on this block."

"What color was it?"

"Dark. Black or navy."

"You didn't write down the license plate by any chance?"

"I tried, but my eye sight's not that good, but they were New York plates. I recognized that much."

"That's very helpful, Mr. Meyers," Mac said.

"So, don't leave an old man in suspense, Mr. Johnson. What's going on that someone who drives a Mercedes would be watching your house?"

"It's a long story, Mr. Meyers," Mac stated. "The bottom line is that some not very nice people might be looking for me and I don't want them to find me. Unfortunately, they may have done so."

"Oy vey! What are you going to do about it?"

"Good question. I'm not sure yet, but if you see anything else again will you call me? Here's my phone number. The phone was just installed the other day."

"Lt. Sheridan is not in," said the person who answered the phone at the New York State Police. "Can I take a message?"

Mac left his name and number, asking that Sheridan get back to him as soon as possible. He feared once he'd been found, whoever wanted him dead would not wait very long to act. What should he do while waiting for Sheridan to call back? Not be alone! He decided to call Denise Richardson.

"You're in luck, Mac," Richardson said when he got her on the phone. "I'm off today because they switched me back to the 7 to 3 shift starting tomorrow."

"Thank goodness," Mac replied.

"I'm glad you approve. So, to what do I owe the pleasure of this call?"

Mac had to make up something quickly. "You have a car, right?"

"Sure do."

"I'm low on groceries and I wondered if we could shop for some groceries if I offer to pay for your dinner?"

"I'd be glad to take you to the supermarket, but you don't have to buy me dinner."

"Then, how about if I pay for the gas?" Mac suggested.

"I've got a better idea," Richardson said. "I've got some home made pasta sauce in the refrigerator. How about if I pick you up right now and we eat here. Then we can get your groceries after dinner?"

Mac hesitated. It was only 3:15. He didn't want to miss Lt. Sheridan's callback. "Denise. I'm expecting an important phone call sometime within the next hour. Can I call you when I've received it and you pick me up then?"

Richardson agreed to that plan. Mac decided that if his enemies decided to act, they would most likely wait until nighttime. By then, hopefully, he'd have talked to Lt. Sheridan and the State Police would be providing him the needed protection.

Chapter Twenty-Three

(1:30 P.M., Same Day)

The phone rang. Mac jumped. He picked it up.

"Mac, it's Lt. Sheridan. I understand you wanted to talk to me? Did you remember something about your past?"

"No. Well, I did have a vague recollection the other night, but nothing significant."

"So, you still don't recall how you ended up in that ditch?"

"I don't."

"Or why you were emaciated and suffering from sensory deprivation when you were rescued?"

Mac was taken aback. "Sensory deprivation? That's the first time I've heard that mentioned."

"One of the doctors included that in his diagnosis."

Mac thought about what that might mean.

Sheridan interrupted his thoughts. "If you didn't recall anything new, how can I help you?"

Mac hesitated. Was he doing the right thing? "I think the person who tried to kill me has found me. I'm afraid he'll try again."

"Explain."

Mac repeated what his neighbor had told him.

"Have you seen the car yourself?" Sheridan asked.

"No, I haven't, but––"

"Have you seen anyone who didn't seem to belong

to the neighborhood, walking or in a vehicle?"

"No."

"Is there anyone outside now?"

"I'll have to put the phone down," Mac replied. He went to the front room. None of the cars parked across the street fit Arthur Meyer's description or appeared to have someone sitting in the driver's seat watching his house.

"I'll contact the Gloversville police," Sheridan said when Mac reported that he saw no suspicious vehicles on the block, "but what would really help is having a license plate number."

"What if he comes back at night?" Mac asked, voicing his worst fear.

"Don't open the door to strangers. If you see one or more suspicious looking people on your block, call 911 right away."

"Don't you think I should go where they can't find me?"

"That's up to you. I know this is not what you want to hear, but you haven't given me enough information to put you under protection."

What does he want--a dead body? "Okay. I'll let you know if he returns or if I can get the license plate."

"Good, and, if you remember anything more, anything that can give us a clue to who you are and what happened to you, please call right away."

"Oh, Lieutenant," Mac said. "Did Bernard Floer call you?"

"Yes. I was out. He left a message, but I haven't had a minute to call him back. Why?"

"He visited me the other day and he's got some ideas that I think you ought to consider."

"Fine. I'll try him this afternoon."

Now what? Mac sat at his kitchen table trying to decide what to do given that the State Police were not about to provide him immediate protection. He couldn't afford a motel and didn't know whether Social Services would pay for one. He could ask Denise Richardson if he could stay at her house, but what if she didn't believe him, or what if she thought he was unstable or even predatory?

He decided to take Denise up on her offer of a meal and a trip to the store. That would give him more time to come up with a plan.

He had forgotten to tell Lt. Sheridan that he remembered something about his past. To prepare for the bookkeeping test, he'd checked out a textbook from the Gloversville library. The material was pretty easy and he was going through it quickly. He knew the terms and the math was rudimentary.

It happened the previous afternoon. When he'd closed the book, he suddenly remembered sitting at another kitchen table with a stack of papers. They were financial documents like the ones in the bookkeeping book, but the numbers were not adding up. He remembered telling someone--could it have been his wife--that he wasn't signing off on something that didn't add up.

He'd told Dr. Bhatt about it during his visit to the hospital that morning. The doctor had seemed pleased. He advised Mac to have a pen and paper ready at all times to write down those memories as they came back to him. Then, they could talk about what he recalled during their visits and perhaps their discussions would trigger additional memories.

Peter G. Pollak

Chapter Twenty-Four

(6:00 P.M., Same Day)

"You seem distracted," Denise said after a lull in the dinner conversation. Mac had been tense from the moment she'd picked him up. She wondered if she was making him nervous, perhaps by not being clear about her motives for befriending him. She decided it was better to ask than worry.

Mac put down his fork. "Do I? I apologize." He hesitated. "There is something on my mind, but I don't want to burden you with my problems."

"I guess that depends on what's bothering you."

He nodded. "True."

"Maybe you could tell me and I'll tell you whether I feel burdened."

"Are you sure you want to know?" Mac asked.

"Unless you're going to tell me you're some kind of serial killer," she replied half seriously.

"No, my gosh. It's nothing like that. I guess I'd better explain. Here it is: I think the people who tried to kill me have found out where I live."

"Ohhh. That is something to be worried about. Have you told anyone else? The Police?"

"I talked to Lt. Sheridan of the New York State Police. He said he'd contact the Gloversville Police Department."

"That's a good start, but what makes you think they've found you?"

"A neighbor saw someone sitting in a car the other day looking at my house."

"Okay, but there are multiple possible explanations for that, right? For example, maybe he was checking out your upstairs neighbor."

"True, except the person who saw this guy says the car left when Mark Weathers picked up me to go to the Employment Office."

"Hmm," Denise said. "That doesn't sound good. Has he been back or has anything else strange happened––like phone call hang ups?"

"No, that's it. I know it's not a lot to go on, but I don't have a lot of options. I don't own a car, I'm virtually penniless and a ten-year old could break into my apartment with a Popsicle stick."

"You're right to be worried, Mac, but you have more options than you think."

Mac looked up. "How do you mean?"

"For one, my younger brother Todd is a Gloversville policeman and for two, you've got me to help you figure out what to do."

"I appreciate all that, Denise. I really do, but what if it's nothing? I don't want to put you or your brother through a lot of unnecessary trouble."

"It's no trouble if we can prevent something bad from happening to you."

Mac looked like he wanted to get up and give her a hug and she almost encouraged him before thinking now's not a good time to get physical.

"Let me call my brother. I think he's working days. He should be home by now."

"Is this an emergency?" Todd McNulty asked after his sister told him she needed him to stop by her house.

"Not one that has to be dealt with in the next ten minutes. Finish your dinner if that's what you're doing."

"We're done, but Tammy went out and I'm supposed to put James to bed. Can it wait until around eight?"

"Not a problem. I'll see you then."

Denise came back to the table. "He's got to wait for his wife to get home. He said he should be here around eight. Let's go get your groceries. Hey, we can even drive past your house and see if that car has returned."

They went to the supermarket, then stopped at Mac's apartment so he could unload his groceries, but the suspicious Mercedes was nowhere to be seen.

"I'm probably just being paranoid," Mac said after they'd returned to her house.

"Nonsense," Denise told him. "Even if it wasn't your attacker, someone did try to kill you and we need to figure out how to keep it from happening again."

Mac could see the family resemblance between Denise Richardson and her younger brother Todd. Studying them, he realized how handsome she was. She had a broad face, wavy brunette hair that she kept short, and eyes that sparkled when she smiled.

Mac could tell her brother was a cop from the way he carried himself. He kept a stern look on his face while Mac and Denise took turns going over the short history of his life since being rescued from gulley in the Adirondacks.

"So that's why I think someone tried to kill me," Mac said, "and why I have been nervous ever since my neighbor told me about someone watching my house."

"You did the right thing contacting the State Police, Mr. Johnson," Todd said. "They've got jurisdiction on your case unless something happens locally that would involve us. But that said, I think I can help you with a few of your issues. For example, I'd be glad to inspect your apartment and write down some recommendations you could give to your landlord."

"That would be helpful," Mac said.

"But that could take days," Denise interjected. "By then, these people could have broken in and you know…finished what they started."

"True," Todd replied. "Can you spend a few nights someplace else until the security work is done?"

"I can't afford a motel or something like that."

"You can stay here," Denise said. "I've got a spare bedroom."

Mac shook his head. "First of all, I don't want to impose and, secondly, I don't want to compromise your reputation."

Denise laughed. "My reputation is probably already compromised beyond repair. Plus, I'm helping a friend in need. So, let's go back to your place so you can get your things."

"What do you think Todd?" Mac asked.

"It's up to Denise. I've long since given up telling her what to do."

Chapter Twenty-Five

(9:00 P.M., Same Day)

Paul Gustafsson called Dr. Plentikov at his home as soon as C.J. Flint's nightly report came off the fax machine. "Flint reports that the patient is starting to remember things."

As usual, Stoner's medical director took a few moments to respond. "Did he say anything about us?"

"No. It was some memory apparently triggered by his studying a book about bookkeeping."

"Bookkeeping? Well, no matter," Plentikov said. "That means it's time to act. I'll have a plan ready when I get there in the morning."

"There's more," Gustafsson said.

"Okay. Give it to me."

"You were spotted."

"Really," Plentikov said. "How interesting."

"This comes from MacVean. The State Police contacted the Gloversville Police to let them know that their mystery man reported that someone in a dark blue or black Mercedes was seen sitting in the car outside his house the other morning."

"I see. They didn't get my license plate, did they?"

"No. If they had, I'm sure you would have heard from them by now."

"True. Okay. It doesn't matter. I saw enough to come up with a plan to retrieve our patient."

"How?" Gustafsson asked.

"I'll tell you in the morning. Be here nine A.M. sharp."

Chapter Twenty-Six

(9:30 A.M., Tuesday, January 31, 2006)

"Call for you, Lieutenant...Says he may have a lead on the mystery man from the Adirondacks."

Bill Sheridan pushed aside the draft of the report he'd been trying to edit since early that morning and picked up the phone. "Sheridan here."

"Lieutenant. This is Bernard Floer––the man who discovered the Adirondacks mystery man."

Damn, I was supposed to call him. Good thing he called me. "Sure. I remember who you are."

"I think he may have been a patient at a place called Stoner Sanitarium."

"Why's that?"

"There are only three year-round institutions within two hours drive of the location where his body was found. I figured that no one who wanted to dispose of a body would drive much farther than that given that there must be dozens of remote locations where you could leave a body to choose from."

"Okay," Sheridan said. "Then why do you say it's this Stoner place?"

"The other two are religious centers. I called both of them and they said no one had gone missing as far as they knew from either their year-round staff or their visitors."

"So you concluded it had to be the hospital?"

"Well, I suppose one of the religious places could be trying to cover something up," Floer said, "but it's not likely. I called the hospital and they refused to answer my questions."

"That's not surprising. They aren't allowed to give out information about patients."

"I understand, but isn't it worth checking out?"

"Maybe," Sheridan said. "Did you ask Mac Johnson about this facility?"

"Yes, and get this––at first he denied having heard the name, but then he told me he had a vague recollection of having seen it someplace. He couldn't remember where, but I thought that was enough of a positive that you might want to check it out."

"I guess it wouldn't hurt to send someone up there. Give me what you know about the place, starting with their full name and address."

Floer had researched Stoner on the web. They didn't have a website, but the name cropped up in a report issued by the New York State Health Department listing private facilities that housed mental health patients. The report listed the address of the facility and the name of its medical director.

"The medical director sounds like he's Russian or Polish," Floer told Sheridan after the latter wrote down the address and phone number. "His name is Dr. Viacheslav Plentikov."

"Okay. I'll check it out. Thanks for the tip," Sheridan said.

Sheridan debated whether to call the facility, go there himself or send someone else. Given the location, it would be a full-day trip from his office in Albany and, taking his current caseload into account, it would be at least a week before he would have a chance to get up there. He decided to call Sergeant Jerzinski who was based at the State Police unit in Glens Falls and ask her to do it. Then, if necessary, he could do a follow-up visit.

Peter G. Pollak

Chapter Twenty-Seven

(4:45 P.M., Same Day)

"Ready?" C.J. Flint asked Paul Gustafsson as he pulled into the driveway of the house where Mac Johnson was reportedly living.

Gustafsson nodded.

Flint turned off the engine and got out of the car. Gustafsson followed. It was four-thirty in the afternoon. The building layout was exactly as Dr. Plentikov had described. The front door opened into a small foyer. Gustafsson stood where he couldn't be seen while Flint rang the first floor doorbell.

They had watched the house for three quarters of an hour, but had not seen any movement. Lights, however, were on in two downstairs rooms.

There was no answer. Gustafsson listened for sounds that indicated someone was inside. Nothing.

Flint rang the bell a third time.

"He's not home," a woman called down from the second floor.

Flint went to the bottom of the stairs. "Do you know where he is?"

"Who's asking?"

"I'm from the hospital," Flint said. He held up a white pharmacy bag. "He needs to start a new prescription."

"You can leave it by the door," the woman said.

Flint looked back to Gustafsson. He shook his head.

"We're not allowed to do that," Flint replied. "Hospital rules."

"Suit yourself," the woman said.

Gustafsson waited until he heard the door close before moving. He wondered if the woman had seen both of them go into the building. "Go," he instructed Flint pointing to the outside. "Get in the car and drive around the corner and wait for me. I'm going to have a look around."

Flint did as instructed. Gustafsson followed him down the front steps, but stayed by the side of the house where he couldn't be seen if someone was looking out of a second story window. He waited in the shadows for a few minutes after Flint pulled out of the driveway, then moved slowly along the side of the house. He stopped by the single first floor window on that side of the house.

The window shade was pulled down but it didn't fit against the glass. The room on the other side of the glass looked to be the bathroom. The door to the room was open slightly, but he couldn't see what lay beyond. He waited a few minutes but could not detect any movement or sign that suggested that Stoner's escaped patient was in the apartment.

He ducked under the window and walked slowly to the back of the house. The snow had been shoveled from the back door to the driveway. Gustafsson walked in a crouch cautiously up to the backdoor. He could see into the kitchen. The overhead light was on, but there was no one in the room.

"He wasn't there," Gustafsson told Dr. Plentikov after C.J. Flint took him back to the Wal-Mart parking lot where he'd left his car, "but he must be using some kind of timer to turn the lights on to make it seem like someone's there."

Plentikov swore. "So where is he? Does Flint have any ideas?"

"Hold on. I'll ask.

Gustafsson covered the phone while he talked to Flint. A couple of minutes later he had an answer. "It seems one of the nurses got pretty friendly with our John Doe. It's possible they've hooked up."

Plentikov snickered. "So, he might just be shacking up with this nurse and has no idea how close he is to coming back here?"

Gustafsson chuckled. "Could be."

"Check it out."

"Tonight?"

"Yes, Mr. Gustafsson. I want you to check it out tonight. Call me if he's there. We still may be able to use the prescription ruse to bring him out into the open."

"Will do."

Gustafsson called Plentikov back a little over an hour later. "We found him. He's in the nurse's house all right. They're watching TV in her living room like a pair of lovebirds."

"Good," Dr. Plentikov said. "That means he hasn't remembered anything that has gotten the attention of the State Police. But we need to move quickly. How secure is the house?"

"Unfortunately, it's pretty damn secure. ADT signs all over the place. She's even got a camera facing the backyard. I had to crawl through two snowy backyards to get a decent view through a side window."

"That's too bad. Okay. Here's what I want you to do. The nurse will have to go to work at some point tonight or tomorrow, leaving our patient alone. Watch the house. When you see her leave, send Flint up to the house."

"With the prescription bag?"

"No. I've got a better idea. Have Flint tell our John Doe that he needs to come to the hospital for a blood test and that his nurse friend gave him the address."

"Okay. Then what?"

"Listen and I'll explain. When he's talked the patient into the car, have him drive to a secluded spot where you'll be waiting. All you need to do is stick a needle in his neck like I showed you and he won't be any trouble. You've got the syringe kit handy, right?"

"Of course. It's right in my pocket."

"Good. Have Flint find out the nurse's work schedule. That way, you can time it properly. Call me as soon as you have him."

"Will do, boss."

Chapter Twenty-Eight

(7:00 A.M., Wednesday, February 1, 2006)

The next morning Denise dropped Mac off at his apartment on her way to work. He needed to check his telephone for messages from the employment office and he'd forgotten to bring the bookkeeping book when he'd picked up his things the previous night. He wanted to keep studying it until the day he would be tested.

No one had left him a message, but Mr. Corwin from the Employment Office called at 8:45. They wanted him to take the bookkeeping exam at 10 A.M. the next morning. Mac said he'd be there.

Mark Weathers from Social Services called fifteen minutes later to convey the same information and to offer to give Mac a ride. Mac agreed. He decided it would be easier for Denise to drop him off at his apartment the following day than to explain to Weathers why he was staying at someone else's house.

Denise had given Mac the option of finding his way back to her house that morning or staying in his apartment until she was off work later that day. Mac didn't think his enemies would try something during daylight hours, but he wasn't entirely comfortable staying in the apartment. In the end, he told Denise he'd take a bus down to the library where he'd continue working with the bookkeeping text and where he could look for a more advanced book when he finished the first one. She agreed to pick him up there after her shift ended at three thirty that afternoon.

Mac was pouring himself a cup of tea when there was a knock on the front door.

Mac froze. Run. Go out the back door.

He tried to calm his nerves. Don't panic he told himself. He walked quietly to the door, secured the chain latch so whoever was on the other side couldn't burst into the room, then opened the door.

"It's me, Mr. Johnson." It was Mrs. Kohler.

"Oh, sorry," Mac said, undoing the chain. "How can I help you today?"

"You had a visitor last night."

"Really. Did you see who it was?"

"He said he was from the hospital and that he had a prescription for you. I thought you ought to know."

A prescription? From the hospital? That didn't sound right.

"Thank you, Mrs. Kohler. I appreciate you're telling me. By the way, did you see what kind of car he was driving?"

"Oh, I'm not good with cars," she replied. "It was a sedan, an older model, I think."

"What color?"

"It was dark by then. So I couldn't tell. Sorry."

"No, that's okay. Thank you."

He supposed it was possible that the hospital had sent over a new prescription for him. He'd just seen Dr. Bhatt the other day, and he hadn't said anything about changing his medications, but…on the other hand, what if it was someone pretending to be from the hospital.

Mac thought of calling Denise and asking her to find out, but he'd have to leave a message since she couldn't take calls while on duty. Better yet, he could call Dr. Bhatt's office. Even if the doctor wasn't available, the

department secretary should be able to look up
something like that.

A half an hour later Mac left his apartment and
started walking towards the bus stop at as rapid a pace
as he could given that his right leg was still weaker than
his left. The fact that some people barely cleared their
sidewalks didn't help. He was in a hurry because Dr.
Bhatt's office denied that they'd sent someone to his
house with a new prescription. He didn't want to be
home if whomever had been there the night before came
back.

Mac wondered if Sheridan would believe him now?
Damn. He should have called him before he left the
apartment. He stopped and turned around, ready to go
back and make the call. But, wait! A dark sedan pulled
into the driveway by his house.

Mac hesitated. What if it's them? He turned and
resumed walking away from his house as fast as he
could. He wanted to run but they'd be less likely to
notice if walked at a normal pace. Maybe they hadn't
spotted him yet.

When he reached the corner, Mac looked back
towards his house. The suspicious car had backed out of
the driveway and was coming in his direction.

He crossed the street as quickly as he could and
entered the corner store breathing heavily. "Can I use
your phone? It's an emergency," he told the woman
behind the counter.

The woman, who acted like she owned the store and
perhaps did, looked at him suspiciously. "What's the
emergency?"

"Someone's after me. They want to kill me."

"Oh yeah? Where are they?"

"They're coming this way. Please. I really need to call 911."

"Listen," she said. "This phone is not for customers. There's a pay phone two blocks down the street. Use that one."

Mac didn't want to go back outside. He wasn't sure what to do.

"Mister, if you're not going to buy something you need to leave," the woman told him.

Mac looked out the front door. There was no sign of the dark car, but that didn't mean they weren't searching for him. Just then, he saw a city bus coming down the street. *Good. I'll go to the library.*

He left the store quickly and limped over to the bus stop, his heart beating a mile a minute. Don't let them see me, he prayed.

Chapter Twenty-Nine

(10:15 A.M., Same Day)

"There he is." Paul Gustafsson pointed to a man getting on the Gloversville city bus.

"Where?" C.J. Flint demanded as he eased the 1993 Pontiac Grand Prix around the corner onto Main Street.

"He just got on that bus."

Flint stepped on the gas.

"Stay back a bit," Gustafsson commanded. "We want to see where he goes when he gets off."

The bus eased up Main Street pulling over every block or so to take on and let off passengers. Finally, at the East Fulton bus stop, Gustafsson saw the man they were after exit the bus. "There he is."

Their prey stood there looking around. Then, he seemed to recognize their car because he hurried to the corner, and with the light in his favor, crossed the street.

"Damn," Gustafsson said. "I think he spotted us. Take a left when the light changes."

Gustafsson lost sight of their prey for a few seconds but picked him up again when they were able to turn onto East Fulton. "Go slowly," he told Flint.

The man kept turning around and looking back as he walked the long block away from Main Street. When he got to the intersection of Main and Fremont, he crossed with the light and went into the large grey stone corner building.

Gustafsson pointed to the building. "What's in there?"

"Public library," Flint replied.

"He went inside."

"Now what?"

"Park the car. I'm going in after him."

When the traffic light turned green, Flint continued up the street and then turned into the library parking lot. "Use the side entrance," he told Gustafsson. "You might be able to surprise him."

The security man got out of the car. Had John Doe gone into the building to call the police? He'd have to keep an ear pealed for sirens. "Stay here, but be ready to move if I come out fast. I'll call you if I need you inside."

Flint nodded. "Got it."

"And, park facing out in case we need to get away quickly," Gustafsson instructed.

Gustafsson removed Dr. Plentikov's medical kit from his pocket and loaded the syringe with the sedative he'd been instructed to use to subdue the patient. He stopped outside the parking lot entrance to the library. He peered through the glass door but couldn't see his man.

He entered the library cautiously. A woman was using the public pay phone. Good. That meant his prey hadn't been able to make any calls. Gustafsson worried that John Doe would make a fuss if he recognized him. He walked cautiously towards the front of the building.

The library was smaller than he'd expected. There were rows of stacks in the center room. He checked each aisle. He came to the Periodical Room, which was crowded. A row of computers along the wall was fully occupied. Several people sat at nearby tables––probably waiting their turn, but there was no sign of John Doe.

He went back into the main room and pretended to

be looking for a book, taking his time checking each aisle. Where is he hiding? There was a second floor but Gustafsson didn't want to go up there in case John Doe spotted him and made for the exit.

Gustafsson tried the men's room. It was empty. He walked back towards the Periodical Room. He noticed someone sitting at a table in the back of the room holding a newspaper so that his face couldn't be seen. That might be him.

Gustafsson pretended to look at the magazines on the display rack that ran the length of the room. When he reached the back section he picked out one and pretended to read it. He slowly turned. It was his man.

How could he get him out of there without stirring up a hornet's nest?

The man turned and looked at Gustafsson, put down the newspaper, got up and started towards the exit.

Gustafsson dropped the magazine and followed. The man walked past the front desk and turned towards the back of the library. Good. Now I've got you.

Gustafsson caught up with him outside the men's room. He grabbed the man's arm and steered him through the restroom door. "Stay quiet and I won't hurt you," he said in a low voice.

"Who are you? What do you want?" the man demanded. There was fear in his eyes.

"I just want to talk. Let's go outside."

"No," the man said loudly. He tried to loosen Gustafsson's grip on his arm. "Let go of me."

Gustafsson slammed the man up against the wall, twisting his arm behind him.

"Help. Help."

Gustafsson had the syringe in his hand. He flicked off the cover and jabbed it into the man's neck.

It was over in a matter of seconds. The escaped patient slumped to the floor. Gustafsson locked the bathroom door and waited a minute to see if someone would come to investigate the noise. No one did.

He took out his cell phone and called Flint. "Come inside. I'll be outside the men's room."

Stoner's security chief waited outside the restroom door. He had to discourage a young man with long stringy hair from entering. "There's someone in here who's sick," he said. "I'm waiting for a friend to take him to the hospital."

The young man gave him a knowing look and went back into the main reading room. Seconds later, Flint came in the back door.

"In here," Gustafsson said, holding the door for Flint.

They each grabbed John Doe by an arm, lifted him up and walked him out of the bathroom, out the back door and towards Flint's car.

"Move," Gustafsson said, after they deposited their victim in the back seat. Flint wheeled out of the parking lot into the street without looking to see if any cars were coming and gunned the engine.

"Where to?" Flint asked.

"We need to transfer him to my car," Gustafsson answered. "Do you know of a quiet place where we can do that?"

"Sure."

"Take me to my car in the Wal-Mart parking lot. I'll follow you."

Thirty minutes later, John Doe was lying on the back seat of Gustafsson's Dodge Charger with his hands strapped behind him. "I've got him," he said when he finally got through to Dr. Plentikov at Stoner.

"Excellent," Plentikov replied. "Bring him here."

Gustafsson handed an envelope with $5,000 cash to C.J. Flint for his role in the kidnapping and told him to keep his mouth shut if he wanted any future work.

"Sure thing," Flint replied after greedily counting the money. "I ain't no rat."

Gustafsson wasn't convinced of that fact, but that wasn't his present concern. Before he drove back into the Adirondacks to deliver John Doe to Dr. Plentikov, he dialed Everett Lipton's direct line at Tekram Corp headquarters. "I've got him."

"Nice work," Lipton said. "Now what?"

"Dr. P hasn't told me."

"Call me as soon as he does."

Peter G. Pollak

Chapter Thirty

(2:45 P.M., Same Day)

Mac woke up on the back seat of a moving car. He was lying face down, his hands tied behind his back, his mouth taped. He felt nauseous. He remembered the car that followed him from his apartment to the library and the man who pushed him into the men's room. He remembered the needle going into his neck.

He lay there fighting the car's motion, trying not to retch.

He rolled over onto the car floor. He couldn't see much out the windows--trees and the occasional telephone poll. Where were they taking him?

The car's driver looked over the seat. "Woke up, eh! We'll be there soon."

Mac kicked the back of the driver's seat.

"Knock that off."

Mac kicked it again.

"I'm warning you."

Mac considered his options. He had the idea that he'd been too passive in the past. Not this time. Maybe if he distracted the driver enough he'd start swerving and attract a cop. Mac kicked the back of the driver's seat once more.

"Do you want another dose of Versed?"

Mac tried to kick out the back window.

His abductor sped up. He seemed to be looking for

something. Suddenly the car swerved. They'd left the highway and were on some kind of gravel road. The car stopped. "All right, smart ass. Now you're gonna get what you asked for."

The man got out of the car and opened the backdoor.

Mac twisted around so that he was on his back with his feet facing his abductor.

The man had a syringe in his hand. Lying half on his back, half on his left side, Mac drew his knees up to his chest. His abductor reached for his top leg. Mac kicked the man's hand away.

"Ouch. Fucker!"

His abductor feinted, then grabbed Mac's right leg. He held it down with one hand and flicked the cap off the syringe. Mac kicked out with his left leg, but missed. He tried again, bringing his left heel down on the man's hand.

The man released his leg. "Fuck! Shit!"

The man stepped back from the car. Mac pulled both legs into his chest ready for the next assault. The man put the syringe in his mouth so he could use both hands. He grabbed one of Mac's legs and started to pull him out of the car. Again, Mac kicked his hands away.

The man feinted grabbing at his legs. When Mac kicked out, the man climbed into the car, trying to hold Mac's legs down. He took the syringe out of his mouth.

Mac wasn't ready to give up. He bucked his legs and turned hard to the left knocking the syringe out of the man's hand.

His abductor's face was red. "You son-of-a-bitch!"

He swung a fist at Mac's head, but the blow glanced off Mac's shoulder. Mac tried kicking him again, but missed. His abductor maneuvered farther on top of Mac.

He punched Mac in the chest, then connected with a solid blow to the nose.

Mac was stunned. He fell back. He felt himself being pulled out of the car.

The man stood him up against the car and punched him twice in the stomach.

Mac slumped to the ground. He looked around for help. They were in the back of a building. No cars around.

He felt the needle enter his shoulder

He started to lose consciousness.

He couldn't fight it.

Peter G. Pollak

Chapter Thirty-One

(4:00 P.M., Same Day)

Denise Richardson was a few minutes late to pick up Mac at the Gloversville Public Library. She told Mac to be across the street from the library at three forty five. When she didn't see him, she pulled around the corner and parked in a lot, then walked back up towards the library. Perhaps he lost track of the time and was sitting in the reading room studying his bookkeeping manual.

But, he wasn't in the reading room. She asked the person at the front desk if she'd seen a man of average height with a neat beard wearing a dark blue winter jacket.

"That description fits about half the men who come into this library," the clerk replied, barely looking up from her paperwork.

Denise searched the first floor for a few more minutes, then went back outside. Maybe he'd gone to buy a newspaper or a cup of coffee, but there was no sign of him on the street.

Walking back to her car, she wondered if he'd misunderstood. Perhaps he'd gone to the library earlier in the day and had taken a bus to her house. She'd given him a spare key. That's probably what happened.

When she pulled into her driveway, however, the house was dark. There was no sign of Mac Johnson and no messages on her answering machine.

There was one more possibility––that he was back at his apartment. Maybe he never went to the library. Tired as she felt from a long day at work, Denise nevertheless put her coat and boots back on and went back out to her car. Driving over to the street where Mac lived, she told herself not to be angry with him. He probably had a good excuse and had forgotten that he could leave messages for her at the hospital.

There were lights on in his apartment, but no one answered the doorbell to his apartment or responded when she banged on the door.

"I don't think he's home," came a voice from the second floor.

Denise went to the stairs. A woman was looking over the railing.

"Did you see him go out?"

"Yes, about mid day."

"He was supposed to meet me at the library, but he wasn't there."

"Sorry," the woman said.

Denise looked at her watch. It was nearly five. She felt queasy. "Okay. If he shows up, tell him to call Denise."

"Will do," the woman replied.

Denise drove back to the library. It was past closing time, so if she'd missed him––if he'd been in the bathroom or on some other floor––he'd probably be outside now waiting for her, but there was still no sign of him on the street.

She drove back to her house, fearing the worst.

When she walked into her house, she went right to the phone without taking off her boots or coat.

"Is Todd home? It's Denise," she said when Todd's wife answered their phone.

"Sorry, he's not here. Can I help you with something?"

"I need to speak to him right away. Please have him call me as soon as he gets in."

Denise fixed her dinner, but found she couldn't eat. She was about to call her brother's house again when the phone rang. Maybe it's Mac, she thought. But it wasn't. It was her brother.

"Mac's missing. You've got to help me."

"Whoa. Slow down. Who's missing?"

"Mac––the man I introduced you to yesterday. I left him at his apartment this morning. He was supposed to be at the library when I got off work, but he wasn't there. I checked the building. I checked his apartment. He's gone. They've got him, Todd. They're going to kill him."

"Stay calm. I'll notify the State Police. There's probably a good explanation."

"That's what you said the last time," Denise said remembering it was Todd who told her about her husband's car being found at the train station in Amsterdam. Frank was wanted in connection with some missing funds from his union. Six months later he was arrested in California and was now serving time in a federal prison.

Denise filed for a divorce the day after he disappeared.

Peter G. Pollak

Chapter Thirty-Two

(6:35 P.M., Same Day)

The phone rang. Denise picked it up on the first ring. Let it be Mac. Please. It was her brother.

"We notified the State Police and they're putting out an APB. Lt. Sheridan will probably call you in the next hour or so to ask you some questions. Tell him everything you can remember."

"I'll be here," Denise said.

"Good. The best thing you can do for your friend is to tell them every little thing––"

"I got the picture, Todd," Denise said.

"Okay. I'll let you know as soon as I hear something."

For the second time that day Mac regained consciousness in the back seat of his captor's car. His face and stomach hurt and he was groggy from the second dose of Versed.

Not willing to repeat his failed escape attempt, Mac assessed his situation. With his hands secured behind his back, he swung his feet off the seat onto the floor and managed to push himself up to a sitting position.

The driver noticed. "Awake are we?" he said, looking at Mac in his rearview mirror. "We're almost there. So don't make me stop the car again or this time I won't be so gentle."

Mac didn't answer, but he didn't see any benefit to taking another beating.

He looked out the car window. They appeared to be in a desolate area––probably back in the Adirondacks. Tall snow banks rose on either side of the road. There were no streetlights and no houses with lights on, no signs of civilization.

Mac wondered about his abductor. His face looked familiar, but he couldn't figure out why he knew him.

The tape over his mouth was loose enough for him to talk. "What have you got against me?"

The driver didn't answer.

"Who do you work for?"

"Shut up," the man replied.

"Why are you doing this?"

The man ignored him. Trying to get any information out of the driver was futile. He said they'd reach their destination soon. Maybe he'd find out then what this was all about. It could also mean his last hours were close at hand. It would have been too dangerous for them to kill him back in Gloversville, but there was nothing up here but woods and deserted summer camps. No one to hear the gunshot or his screams.

Five minutes later, the driver turned left into a barely visible driveway. Mac leaned forward to see where they were going. A long driveway wound through the trees. He could begin to see lights through the snow-covered tree branches. Finally, a large stone building appeared. Mac read the name stenciled above the front door. It said Stoner Sanitarium.

Something clicked in Mac's brain. "I've been here before."

"Welcome home," his abductor said with a snarl.

Peter G. Pollak

"This is where they sent me, right?"

"Whatever. Dr. P. is waiting for you."

Dr. P.? Mac remembered a thin-faced, angry man in a white lab coat, standing up behind a large desk giving him a speech. His hands had been tied behind his back like now. Someone was holding him in a chair and the doctor was telling him that he was there for treatment and had better behave. He had tried to protest when the doctor told him he was mentally ill and needed quiet. Mr. Gifford he called me.

"My name is Gifford, Logan Gifford," he said aloud.

"Was," his captor said. "Here your name is John Doe and pretty soon it's going to be 'never laid eyes on him.'"

Suddenly it all came back to him––the conference room and the camera where Zander and Lipton made him lie about defrauding the government. He'd done it to save Debbie and the kids. Then they sent him to this hellhole. And now he was back.

The driver pulled up in front of the building. He took a walkie-talkie out of his glove compartment and told someone that he was there.

I've got to get away, Logan told himself. He'd try when they came to get him out of the car. He'd head-butt the driver and…but he knew as long as his hands were tied behind his back, his chances of getting anywhere were nil. It had been a three-hour drive north of the Thruway the first time when he'd been driven there by Everett Lipton's henchmen.

Maybe, if he got back to the main road, he could flag down a passer by. But what were the chances someone would come along? He'd only seen two cars going the other way during the past fifteen minutes. Worse, it must be approaching nine or ten at the night. Few people would be on the road at this hour.

A man came out of the front door. Logan couldn't see his face. The driver got out of the car and came around to the passenger's side. He opened the door.

"You've got a choice," he said to Logan. "Come out on your own, or if I have to drag you out, I'm going to smash your nose into the driveway and then break every bone in your body one by one just for the fun of it."

"I'm coming," Logan said. He hoped there'd be an opportunity to make a break for it once he was on his feet, but as soon as he was out of the car, his captor threw a black cloth bag over his head. They started walking him forward.

The darkness hit Logan like a runaway train. He began to sweat. His stomach turned over. He couldn't breath. For a second, he wished he were dead. Don't give them the satisfaction he told himself as he was manhandled up a set of steps into the building. Don't give up. No matter what.

Logan tried to concentrate on the echoes of his feet as his abductors walked him into the building, down a corridor. He heard a door being opened. Someone shoved him forward, then pushed him into a chair.

"Well, well. Look who's back home."

Logan recognized the voice. He remembered the day when he'd been in that same chair, listening to the same speaker.

"You can remove the head covering, Paul. I want our visitor to know where he is and what's going to happen to him."

The bag was removed roughly from Logan's head. He had to blink a few times to adjust to the bright desk lamp that was shining in his face. Behind it was the dark outline of his tormentor--Dr. Plentikov.

"Why are you doing this?" Logan said. "I haven't done--"

"Silence," Plentikov yelled. "I'll do the talking here and you'll listen quietly or we'll have to put a gag in your mouth."

"You might as well--"

"Okay. Do it!" Plentikov said, looking at the person to Logan's right.

"You won't get away with this. The State Police--"

A rag pushed into his mouth cut off the rest of his sentence. Logan tried to resist, twisting his head, but Plentikov's men were stronger. Duct tape secured the rag. He gagged as the rag penetrated his throat. The gag was choking him to death.

"Let's not kill him quite yet," Plentikov said.

Someone slapped him on his back. He started to wretch. Someone pulled the gag out of his mouth. Tears streamed out of his eyes as he fought to regain his breath.

"This is what happens to people who try to escape," Plentikov said. "They always come back. But they don't escape a second time. Your quarters are waiting for you. Take him out of my sight."

Logan was pulled to his feet. The bag was placed back over his head. No! He couldn't be in the dark. Not again.

He tried to keep track of the turns and distances as they walked him down a corridor, down a set of stairs, down another corridor and another.

"Open the door."

"What about his hands?"

"What about them?

"And the bag over his head?"

"Getting soft on me, are you?"

"No, I just want to do what the boss--"

"It's up to me and I say, leave it on."

Peter G. Pollak

Chapter Thirty-Three

(7:30 P.M., Same Day)

Logan was shoved forward and fell onto the hard concrete floor. He heard a door close behind him. Then silence. He lay there for a long time, trying to gain control over his emotions. There was little doubt in his mind they intended to kill him. But when? Was there time for someone to rescue him? Who knew where he was? His mind searched wildly for something to hang onto, some hope that his life was not over.

By now, Denise would know that he'd been taken. She would contact her brother who would call the State Police. Could they figure out who had taken him? They hadn't been able to identify him these past six months. Why did he think they'd figure it out now?

He inched back towards where he thought the door was. His foot hit the wall. He turned around and kneeled, then tried to feel for the door. He found a seam in the wall, but no door handle. It was the same windowless padded room they'd kept him in the first time.

He lowered himself to the floor. He had to get the bag off his head.

He rubbed his head against the wall, hunching his shoulders to try to lift it. He managed to slide the bag slightly from one side to the other, but not off.

He rolled over onto his knees and leaned forward in

hopes that the bag would slide off. Finally, by rubbing his head against the wall while on his knees, the bag came off.

Darkness. Total darkness. He screamed and screamed and screamed even though he knew no one could hear him and no one was coming.

Chapter Thirty-Four

(Midnight, Same Day)

Mac didn't know how long he'd been in the room. His mind was playing tricks on him. He imagined he could see things out of the corner of his eye, but then he'd turn his head and nothing. Blackness.

His shoulders and arms were numb. Lying on his side, he tried to slide his arms under his backside, but there wasn't enough leeway.

The floor was rough. Perhaps he could cut the strap by scraping it along the floor.

He maneuvered himself onto his back and rubbed the plastic strap that bound his hands along the floor, but all he succeeded in doing was scrape his hands.

He rolled onto his side. Why? Why me?

He started crying uncontrollably.

Eventually he dozed off.

He heard the door to his cell open. He had no idea how much time had passed. He rolled over. A man stood in the doorway. The light from the hall blinded Logan. Who was it? Were they coming to kill him?

The man turned on the ceiling light. It was Fred. "I brought you some breakfast."

The guard set a tray on the floor by Logan. On it was some toast covered with jam and oatmeal. The guard removed Logan's plastic strap binding his hands. He wasn't hungry, but he appreciated the gesture.

Fred went back outside and brought in some hot tea in a paper cup. "I'll leave the light on while you eat, but then I'll have to turn it off."

"Please," Logan moaned. "The dark. I can't––"

"Okay. I'll leave it on, but when Gustafsson comes back, I've got to turn it off."

"Thank you," Logan said. "Thank you."

Chapter Thirty-Five

(5:30 A.M., Thursday, February 2, 2006)

"What are you doing here so early?" Carol Murphy asked Denise Richardson as the latter appeared at the Intensive Care nurses' station. Denise was not due into work until later that day.

"I'm looking for a phone number," Denise replied. "Remember the guy who saved Mac Johnson's life?"

"I don't think I was on duty when he visited," Carol replied.

Richardson started rooting around her work area. "He gave me his business card and I couldn't find it at home. I thought I might have left it here."

"Why do you need it--if I may ask?"

"I need to get a hold of him. Mac's gone missing and I think Mr. Floer would want to know."

"Gone missing! What--"

"I don't even want to think about what it means, Carol," Denise said.

"Can I help you look?" Carol asked.

"Not necessary," Denise replied. "I just found it."

Denise went out to her car in the hospital parking lot and called the number on Bernard Floer's business card. It rang several times. Then an answering machine picked up. Denise hung up and dialed the number a second time. This time someone answered.

"Hello. Is Bernard Floer there, please?" she asked.

"Do you realize it's barely six A.M.?"

"It's an emergency," Denise replied.

"May I tell Bernard who is calling?"

"My name is Denise Richardson. It's about the man whose life he saved."

"Really? Again."

"Please!" Denise begged.

"Okay. Just a minute."

Denise drummed her fingers on the steering column while she waited. Five minutes went by. Had he hung up on her?

"Hello. This is Bernard Floer."

"Mr. Floer. This is Denise Richardson. You probably don't remember me. I'm a nurse in the critical care unit at Nathan Littauer Hospital in Gloversville."

"Sure, Miss Richardson. What can I do for you?"

"Mac––the man you rescued. He's missing."

"Missing? Oh, God! What happened?"

"I was supposed to meet him yesterday afternoon after work, but he never showed up."

"Did you check his apartment?"

"I did. He isn't there."

"Did you contact the police?"

"I notified the Gloversville Police Department and I'm pretty sure they contacted the State Police."

"What do you think this means, Miss Richardson?"

"As far as Mac's disappearance, I'm afraid it means the people who left him in that gully have come back to finish him off."

"You may be right," Floer said. "He and I talked about that possibility when I visited him last week."

"I'm sorry I woke you up. I'm just beside myself. I feel so helpless," Denise said. "I needed to talk to someone who would understand."

"I certainly do understand," Floer said. "But things

might not be hopeless. I told the State Police the other day about a place that might be involved in this."

"What do you mean?"

"There are only a couple of year-round facilities in the Adirondacks that are within a couple of hours of where Mac was left to die. There are two religious centers and a mental health hospital by the name of Stoner Sanitarium. Have you ever heard of it?"

"Let me think. I believe I saw that name on a list of places in the Adirondacks that our hospital services in emergencies. A helicopter pad was installed at the hospital a few years ago to be able to receive emergency patients that don't need to be taken down to Albany."

"I suggested that the State Police check to see if anyone at any of those three places recognized Mac's photo," Bernard said.

"But wouldn't they have informed the police if someone who was staying there went missing?"

"You'd think so. I agree it doesn't make a lot of sense, but I thought they should check out every possible angle."

"Did you know if they contacted any of them?" Denise asked.

"The investigator––Lt. Sheridan––thanked me, but I didn't get the impression he was going to drop everything and go up there. So, I called all three places myself."

"Good for you," Denise said. "Did you learn anything?"

"The people I spoke with at the religious centers denied any of their residents or visitors had gone missing. The hospital refused to answer any of my questions."

"I know that sounds suspicious, but they have to protect their patients' rights."

"I suppose you're right," Floer said, "But I'm inclined to believe the people from the religious organizations. That leaves the hospital."

"What if someone there was involved in trying to kill Mac?"

"Then he's probably in real danger."

"I know it's far fetched, but I just can't sit around waiting for him to show up dead. I'm going up there."

"Alone?"

"If I have to."

"Denise, can you wait an hour? I'd like to go with you."

Chapter Thirty-Six

(7:50 A.M., Same Day)

Lt. Sheridan sat in the ready room waiting for Al Potter, chief of the Gloversville Police Department, to gather his people. It was ten minutes to eight Thursday morning. Nothing had come in overnight concerning the man known as Mac Johnson.

"The State Police would like our help looking for a missing person," Potter said by way of introduction to his day shift. "Lt. Sheridan is here to give us the details."

Sheridan outlined the facts of the situation, which were few.

"I'm passing out a description with a photo of the victim taken while he was still a patient in your local hospital. I'm told he kept the beard neatly trimmed and that his hair may be a little longer than in the photo. He does not have a car. Nor does he have a driver's license or any identification other than perhaps a library card and a food stamps card."

"He was supposed to be picked up at the Gloversville Library around 4 P.M. yesterday afternoon. Start there. Interview the personnel and patrons to see if anyone remembers having seen him. He probably took the city bus to get there from his apartment. So, someone else ought to check with the drivers on duty yesterday."

Sheridan handed out a slip of paper. "This sheet contains his address, height, weight and other information you can use to identify him as well as my contact information. I'm heading up into the Adirondacks to visit a medical facility to see if he might have been a patient there. If you learn anything at all, please call my office and give them the information. If you find him, dead or alive, call me immediately. We appreciate your help on this. Any questions?"

Sgt. Fiorino raised his hand. "What are the chances that he recovered his memory and decided to split?"

"Good question. The answer is I don't know. I'll be stopping at the hospital on my way north to meet with his doctor. If I learn anything that could be helpful to your search, I'll let you know right away. Anything else?"

"Any idea who is after him?" Fiorino asked.

"At this point we do not. We have not been able to discover his real identity. Therefore, we don't know who his enemies are."

Chief Potter wrapped up the meeting. He assigned a couple of officers to check out the library, the bus company and to talk to people in the neighborhood where Mac Johnson had been living.

Chapter Thirty-Seven

(8:45 A.M., Same Day)

Sgt. Ellen Jerzinski studied the outside of the large stone building. She'd been told it had been built as a tuberculosis sanitarium. Now it was a private mental health hospital. The silent coldness of the building was exacerbated by the minus ten-degree wind chill that the early morning sun had yet to penetrate.

Earlier in the week, Lt. Sheridan asked Jerzinski to check out the possibility that the mystery man she'd interviewed in Gloversville back in October had been a patient at Stoner. She had not been able to free up the time the past two days, but at 6:30 the previous evening Sheridan called to let her know the mystery man was missing and request that she get up there first thing the next morning.

He would head up there as well, he told her, but he had to make a couple of stops in Gloversville. He told her to wait for him after their visit to Stoner in the Village of Meadow Lake at the local Stewart's gas station and convenience store.

Her partner, Ed Collins, opened the car door. "Ready?"

Collins must have hated the drive from Glens Falls. She knew he disliked the religious programs she preferred to listen to while driving. But she was the senior officer and got to decide what stations they listened to. Besides, there weren't that many choices in the Adirondacks in the first place.

The door to the building was locked. Sgt. Jerzinski pushed the buzzer.

"Who is it?" a woman's voice asked.

"New York State Police. We'd like to talk to your medical director."

"Do you have a warrant?"

"We are not here to search your facility. We'd just like to meet with him for a few minutes."

"Hold on. I'll see if he's available."

"They're hiding something," Collins volunteered.

Jerzinski turned to look at him. He turned away. "Could be," she said, turning back to the door.

Collins paced.

The door opened. A middle-aged woman in a nurse's uniform held the door for them.

"Dr. Plentikov is on a very tight schedule today, but he can give you a few minutes," she told them.

They followed the nurse down a corridor. The building was eerily quiet. There were no other people to be heard or seen. The nurse knocked on the door of an office that had a sign that said "Medical Director." A man in medical whites got up from behind the large desk that dominated the room and offered his hand. He had a narrow face with glasses and thin black hair combed behind his ears.

"I'm Dr. Plentikov, Medical Director here at Stoner. How can I help you?"

Sgt. Jerzinski introduced Collins and herself. She took the photo of the mystery man out of her briefcase. "Do you know this man? Has he ever been a patient here?"

Plentikov studied the photo. "Not in my time here and I've been here for more than five years."

"You're sure you've never seen him?" Jerzinski asked. "Maybe he worked here or made deliveries here?"

"In terms of deliveries, I wouldn't know. Other people accept deliveries, but I'd know if he worked here in any capacity and I can assure you that he's never been employed at Stoner."

"Look again," Jerzinski said. "He may not have had the beard."

"I don't have to," Plentikov replied, handing the photo back to her. "I'm positive. Is he a criminal? Are we in any danger from him?"

"No. We'd just like to talk to him. Keep the photo in case he turns up. I've got other copies."

"Very well," Plentikov said. "By the way, if he does show up, where can I reach you?"

Jerzinski gave him her card. She thought about asking for a tour of the building, but Sheridan told her to just ask about the photo and then wait for him.

After they were shown to their car, she drove down the driveway and turned south before pulling over about a mile down the road.

"What do you think?" she asked Collins.

"He was lying," he said.

"Why do you say that?"

"The way he answered. He seemed to know what we were going to ask him."

"I thought so, too. I'll call Sheridan and find out what he wants us to do."

Peter G. Pollak

Chapter Thirty-Eight

(9:15 A.M., Same Day)

Paul Gustafsson's walkie-talkie beeped. "Hold him," he told his assistant Fred, letting go of Logan Gifford's arm to answer the call. They had just removed Gifford from his cell and were halfway up the stairs to the first floor.

It was Dr. Plentikov. "What's up?"

"Change of plans. Put him back in his room and come up here."

"Okay. Got it."

Gustafsson pointed back towards the basement solitary room. "Change of plans."

"What's up?" Fred wanted to know.

"I don't know," Gustafsson replied, "but Dr. P. wants us to put him back in the room. Do you think you can manage that without losing him while I find out what's going on?"

Fred blanched, but nodded. "Sure, boss."

Gustafsson went upstairs and knocked on the Medical Director's office door.

"Enter."

"What's up?"

"We just had a visit from the New York State Police. They wanted to know if I'd ever seen this man," Plentikov replied, shoving the photo they'd left behind across the desk.

"It's him," Gustafsson said.

"I know it's him," Plentikov said. "My question is why did they come here looking for him? Did you leave some loose ends when you picked him up?"

"Not a chance. Did they have anything other than the photo?"

"No. They just asked if I'd seen him and I said 'no.'"

"I doubt if they have anything. They're probably just checking on every institution in a 100-mile radius of where they found him."

"Why now––so long after the fact?"

"Because he disappeared again?" Gustafsson guessed.

Plentikov thought about that for a minute. "You may be right, but whatever the reason, we've got to get rid of him fast––before they come back with a search warrant."

"Okay. How do you want to do it?"

Plentikov got up and went over to an oak cabinet next to a large filing cabinet, took out a bottle of scotch and poured himself a finger and downed it in one swallow. "Killing him is not the problem. The problem is how do we get rid of the body so it can't be traced back to us?"

Gustafsson agreed. "We have to get him off the property that's for sure."

Plentikov came back to his desk and sat down. "But how? What if they're watching everyone who comes and goes?"

"What if I take him out in the trunk of my car at the end of the shift? Are they going to search every vehicle that leaves here?"

"I don't know, but if they stopped your car for whatever reason, our goose would be cooked."

Gustafsson thought for a moment. "There is the

back way." He was referring to an old logging road that dead-ended at the back of the facility's property. It wound through the woods and came out on a side road a mile from the house Gustafsson rented. He bought a snowmobile just so he could ride it over the logging road to work on days when road conditions were bad.

"I hadn't thought of that," Plentikov said. "But how are you going to do it? Knock him out and throw him over the seat in front of you?"

"That's one way, but I have a toboggan back at my place which can be attached to the snowmobile. I can take him out that way."

"Fine. Do it."

"Am I taking him out dead or alive?"

Plentikov walked over to the window and stood with his back to the room. "Let's think about that for a moment. There are plenty of medicines that would do the trick, but if they find the body and do an autopsy, it could point back to us."

Gustafsson sat down in one of the chairs in front of the desk. "Alive then. So, what should I do with him––drop him off into another gully? He can't be lucky twice––especially in the middle of winter."

Plentikov sat back down in his black leather desk chair. He took a breath and blew it out. "I should never have accepted this commission in the first place."

"The money must have been good."

"Not enough to justify these complications. Any ideas?"

Gustafsson wanted Plentikov to offer him a scotch, but knew it would never happen. The man was oblivious to others' needs. "There's a hunting shack half a day's ride from here where Fred and I went hunting last fall. It's on state land. No one but a few hunters ever go up there. If I leave him there with no coat or boots, he'll never make it out alive."

"Sounds good. How far did you say?"

"It'd take me a full day to drive up there, take him into the woods on the snowmobile and then drive back."

"Okay. Do it."

Gustafsson turned to go.

"One second," Plentikov said. "I need you here for the next day or two in case the State Police come back and want to do a search. Can you find some place close by to keep him for a few days? Then when things quiet down you can take him to that shack."

Gustafsson nodded. "There's an old barn in back of an abandoned house on my road. I'll take him up there and leave him tied up."

"Fine, and if he freezes to death, all the better."

Gustafsson went to his office and closed the door. He pulled out his cell phone. Minutes later, he was explaining the situation to Tekram's security chief.

"Why do you think they'll come back?" Gustafsson asked.

"If they think our guy is there, they'll get a warrant," Tekram's Everett Lipton answered. "You'd better move him right away."

"No problem."

"Will Plentikov hold up if the State Police show up again?" Lipton inquired.

"Plentikov's feeling the pressure, but he knows what he's looking at if he slips up. Plus, right now there's nothing to tie your man to Stoner."

"Let's hope you're right. What about the rest of the people who work there? Can we count on them to keep their mouths shut?"

"The only ones who know anything are my men and I've gone over with them what to say."

"Which is what?" Lipton demanded.

"Which is they rarely come in contact with the patients. I told them they're legally responsible for what goes on here so if anyone asks, they need to deny having seen anyone who fits his description."

"What about the nursing staff and the kitchen people?" Lipton asked. "Some of them must have known you were holding an extra person for almost two years."

"Plentikov made it pretty clear to each person he hired that what goes on at the facility stays there. People who live up here are pretty closed-mouthed anyway."

"Okay. Well, you'd better get going. Get Gifford out of that facility and let me know when he's an ice cube."

Peter G. Pollak

Chapter Thirty-Nine

(10:15 A.M., Same Day)

When Fred put Logan back in the padded cell, he didn't re-attach the straps that Gustafsson had used to bind Logan's arms behind him. He also removed the black bag from Logan's head and gave him a bottle of water.

Logan's captor—whose name he now knew was Paul Gustafsson—had informed him matter-of-factly that they were taking him someplace to kill him. Logan doubted that was just a scare tactic. Now that his memory had returned to him, he represented a threat not only to his former company, but also to Dr. Plentikov and Stoner Sanitarium. They had to kill him.

He now understood that his being left in the roadside gully had been an attempt to dispose of him in a way that would not implicate Stoner or Dr. Plentikov. They would have to find a similar solution, which meant they weren't likely to shoot him or poison him. He didn't want to think about what alternative method they had settled on.

Fortunately, Fred had taken pity on him and left the overhead light on. But that was cold comfort.

You're going to die, he told himself. Is there any way you can help the State Police catch your killers? The problem was he couldn't think of any way he could do so. He sat down and drank the water the guard had given him. Both of them would probably be punished when Gustafsson found out.

A thought came to mind. Plentikov must have tried to keep knowledge of his presence to as small a number of people as possible. The more people who knew about him the more likely one of them would break under questioning. He wondered about Fred. The guy seemed to have a conscience. What about the others? He had to take a chance to let them know he was being held there against his will--no matter the consequence.

Suddenly, the overhead light went off. A few seconds later the door opened. In came Fred followed by Gustafsson.

"You left him in here with his hands free?" Gustafsson demanded.

"I don't have any of those straps you use," Fred replied.

"It doesn't matter. Get up," he said to Logan. "You're coming with me."

Logan backed away.

Gustafsson scowled. "You can either cooperate or you can make it difficult for yourself. I don't care."

"You won't get away with this," Logan said. "You've already committed a dozen--"

Gustafsson rushed at Logan, knocking him to the ground. He secured Logan's hands behind him with a pair of plastic strips.

"Help! Someone. Help," Logan yelled.

Gustafsson pulled a roll of tape out of his jacket and taped Logan's mouth shut. "What was that you were saying?" he said laughing.

Chapter Forty

(11:45 A.M., Same Day)

Lt. Sheridan pulled into the parking lot at the local Stewart's gas station and convenience store in the Village of Meadow Lake. He found Sgt. Jerzinski and her partner inside sitting in one of the booths drinking coffee. Sheridan motioned for them to come outside. They got in the back seat of his car.

"So what'd you find?" Sheridan asked.

"The medical director at Stoner denies ever having seen the man in the photo," Jerzinski replied.

"Do you believe him?"

"I have my doubts," she replied, "and Collins here thinks he was lying."

"Why's that?" Sheridan asked.

Collins leaned forward. "Barely looked at the photo. Said 'no' too quickly…as if he knew what we were there for."

"Good observation, but that's not enough to convince a judge to give us a search warrant," Sheridan stated.

"So what's next?" Jerzinski asked.

"State Health Department. They have jurisdiction over the patients. I'll see if we can get them to send a couple of their investigators up here first thing in the morning."

"Would we be allowed to go in with them?" Collins asked.

"Only if the facility agreed and I can't see that they would do so––whether they've got our guy in a padded room or not."

"Okay," said Jerzinski. "If that's all you need from us, we'll head back to Glens Falls."

Sheridan nodded. "Good job. I'll let you know if I need anything else."

Four hours later Sheridan slammed down his office phone. He'd just spent over an hour trying to get the New York State Health Department to send a couple of investigators up to the Adirondacks to inspect the Stoner Sanitarium.

He had talked to five people before reaching someone with the authority to order such an inspection, but Deputy Commissioner Alice Margold wasn't going to act unless Sheridan went through proper channels including submitting paperwork signed by the head of his unit justifying the request.

"That could take days and we've got reason to believe a man's life is in danger," Sheridan told her.

"Put that in your paperwork, Lieutenant," Margold replied before hanging up on him.

He reported his problem to Captain Falcone who sympathized and said he'd expedite the paperwork, but didn't see any way around it.

Sheridan returned to his office to start filling out the forms. The sad part about it he knew was that it would be his ass that would be in a sling if Mac Johnson ended up dead.

Chapter Forty-One

(12:30 P.M., Same Day)

"Quite a place," Denise Richardson remarked as they drove up the long driveway to Stoner Sanitarium's main entrance.

"It was built almost one hundred years ago," Bernard Floer answered. "I understand it was closed during World War II and remained empty for more than a decade until someone decided it would be the perfect place to treat rich patients with mental health issues."

"Must cost a fortune to heat," Denise said as they pulled into the sole visitor's parking spot.

Ten minutes later they were seated in the visitors' waiting room having told the woman who opened the front door that they were a professional photography team who wanted to take some photos of their facility for a study of former tuberculosis sanitaria in the Adirondacks.

Fifteen minutes later the receptionist returned with a man wearing a security uniform.

"I've spoken with our director and he says that he can't permit you to take any pictures of the inside."

"Why's that?" Bernard asked.

"Patients have the right to privacy, Mr. Floer," she answered. "But if you want to take some pictures of the outside of the building you may do so, but just for an hour. Fred Daniels here will show you around."

"What about parts of the inside where there are no patients?"

"I'm sorry sir," she replied. "Dr. Plentikov was very clear. He will not permit any photos of the inside of the facility."

"I see," Bernard said.

"Do you want to take photos of the outside or not?" the receptionist asked.

"Yes, I do," Bernard replied.

"We can only allow you on the grounds for one hour," the woman stated. "Then you'll have to leave."

Bernard looked at Denise. She nodded her consent. There was no point in arguing. An hour was better than nothing.

It had been Bernard's idea to use his profession to try to gain access to the facility. "If they are holding Mac, do you think they'll admit it if we walk up to the front door and ask to see him?"

Denise had to admit that he was right.

"Hopefully, we can at least get a feel for the kind of facility they're running," Denise said, "including what kind of security they have."

"What are you thinking?" Bernard asked. "I hope you don't plan to break into the place."

Denise laughed. "Let's hope it doesn't come to that," she said. "We just need to find something that will convince the State Police he's there."

"That sounds more like what I had in mind."

The security guard seemed ill at ease. Bernard told the man he needed to walk around for a few minutes to decide the best locations for him to take the pictures. He alternately hovered close or stayed far away from them as Bernard tested light conditions with his meters.

Denise pretended to be his assistant since that was how Bernard explained her role to the receptionist. She carried one of Bernard's equipment bags and made suggestions for locations to take his photos.

Given that it was the middle of winter and the snow banks were over five feet high, they had to stick to areas that had been cleared of snow. That left out the northern side of the building. The driveway extended along the side facing south. Denise followed Bernard as he walked around to the back of the building.

The driveway was widened out into spots for staff parking and access to a three-car garage. The doors to all three garage bays were open. Vans with the name Stoner Sanitarium on the sides were parked in two of the bays. The third contained a dark-colored Mercedes Benz with New York license plates.

Hadn't Mac mentioned that the car the neighbor had spotted casing his house was a Mercedes? She almost said something to Bernard, but realized the security guard would overhear. Instead without looking directly at the car she moved closer to it so she could memorize the license plate number.

Bernard set up his tripod and camera and started taking some pictures of the back of the building. Denise continued to walk around the cleared out area. As she turned to go back to where Bernard was working, she noticed a matted down path along the northern side of the garage. It looked like a cross-country ski trail or one used by snowmobiles. "Where does that lead to?" she asked the guard who had been following a few feet behind her.

"There's an old logging trail back there," he explained. "Mr. Gustafsson uses it sometimes to come to work on his snowmobile."

"Who's Mr. Gustafsson?"

The man looked uncomfortable. "I'm not sure I should say."

"Why not? Did someone tell you not to?"

"No, not exactly."

Denise put her hands on her hips. "Well then?"

"I guess you could look it up. He's the Director of Security here."

"Thank you," Denise stated.

Bernard was taking photos from the side of the building when the receptionist came outside with her coat on. "Yoo-hoo," she called. "Your hour is up. It's time for you to leave."

Bernard continued to shoot different angles, making the woman come up the driveway towards where they were standing.

"Certainly," he said when she called a third time. "We're just about done anyway."

A while later they were driving down the driveway towards the state highway.

"I don't know whether that was worthwhile," Bernard said. "What do you think?"

"I think it was very worthwhile," Denise said.

"Really?"

"Indeed. First, I got the license plate off a Mercedes Benz that was parked in the garage."

"Why is that significant?"

"Mac must not have told you, but a neighbor told him that someone seemed to be casing his building. The person couldn't read the license plate but he said it was a Mercedes Benz and the car had a New York license plate."

"Coincidence?"

"I'd say that would be enough for the State Police to want to investigate."

"Good. Anything else?"

"It may be nothing, but there's a snowmobile trail going back towards the woods that supposedly is used by the Director of Security--a Mr. Gustafsson."

"Also, interesting," Bernard said, "but in and of itself it doesn't prove anything."

"True, but it means they have more than one way to move people in and out of the facility."

"So what do we do now?" Floer asked.

"Call my brother. He'll get in touch with the State Police investigator whose leading the search to find Mac."

Peter G. Pollak

Chapter Forty-Two

(1:45 P.M., Same Day)

Paul Gustafsson's cell phone went off. It was Everett Lipton. Just what he needed—someone else telling him what to do.

He was on his way back to Stoner, having secured Logan Gifford to a toboggan behind his snowmobile and having transported him that way to an old barn behind an abandoned house not far from his rental property.

Having decided he wanted Gifford to still be alive when he dropped him off in the middle of the Adirondacks with no means of survival for the pleasure of watching him plead for his life, Gustafsson had ordered the prisoner to put on an old snowsuit and ill-fitting boots that he'd found in Stoner's supply room. After securing him to a post in the barn, he even left Gifford a couple of sandwiches and two bottles of water from Stoner's kitchen.

Gustafsson intended to return once a day to make sure his prisoner was still alive. Then, when the coast was clear, he would transport him miles farther into the woods where he would leave him to freeze to death. If the body were ever found, there'd be no evidence connecting him to Stoner.

"What's up?" he asked Lipton.

"That's what I'd like to know," Lipton replied. "What have you done with you know who?"

Gustafsson briefed him on the current situation.

"And how is the good doctor holding up?" Lipton wanted to know.

"He'll be fine as long as he never has to see your guy again," Gustafsson replied.

"Even if the State Police return?"

"Unless they have some evidence I don't know about."

"Good. That's what I like to hear," Lipton said. "Let me know when you've disposed of the body."

Chapter Forty-Three

(2:30 P.M., Same Day)

"Shouldn't we wait for the State Police?" Bernard Floer asked Denise Richardson who was picking out a snowsuit in the local snowmobile rental shop in the Village of Meadow Lake.

It had been her idea after she put in the call to her brother to report the results of their visit to Stoner to rent a snowmobile and explore the trail that Stoner's chief of security used to access the back of the facility.

"We've no idea when the State Police will get here," Denise replied, "and, if we find where they're holding him, we can save them time and perhaps save Mac's life."

Bernard's eyebrows arched. "Are you sure you know how to drive one of these things?"

"Positive. I'm the only girl in a family with three brothers who wouldn't let me stay home and play with dolls. Now, have you picked out a snowsuit in your size?"

An hour later they were headed back north towards Stoner Sanitarium pulling a two-seater on a trailer behind Floer's SUV.

"How do we access the trail?" Bernard asked. "I'm sure they won't let us drive onto Stoner's property, park our car and hop on the trail."

"Of course not," Denise said, "but there's no need.

The snowmobile shop gave me a map showing all the public trails in the county. There's a place we can access the logging road about three miles north of Stoner's entrance. There's even a place to park your car."

Bernard continued to drive cautiously along the winding highway, never having pulled a snowmobile trailer behind his SUV before. Denise had offered to drive, but he decided he was being a namby-pamby and at least could do the driving.

He was still doubtful about their trying to find Logan on their own, however. It seemed like trying to find an open gas station in upstate New York after midnight.

Twenty minutes later Denise pointed out the parking area that gave them access to the snowmobile trail that connected to the logging road that dead-ended behind Stoner Sanitarium.

"Don't forget to bring your camera bag," Denise said. "You might be able to get some photos that can be used as evidence."

"I'm with you," Bernard replied.

Denise laughed. "You've got a telephoto lens, right?"

"Of course."

Bernard was surprised at the size of the snowmobile they'd rented. He didn't know how they would be able to get it off the trailer, but Denise made it look easy. She extended a ramp from the back of the trailer, got on the snowmobile, started it up and drove it down the ramp.

Minutes later Bernard was sitting on the back of the machine.

"These things are pretty loud," Denise said before getting on in front of Floer. "If you need to talk to me, just tap me on the shoulder. Ready?"

Bernard wasn't sure. *I must be crazy.* "We've come this far. I guess we might as well see what we can find."

"There's Stoner," Denise yelled back to Bernard as they came over a rise. The large structure looked more institutional from the back than the front, but it was still an imposing site in the middle of a forest of seventy-five foot tall snow-covered pines. It had only taken half an hour to backtrack from where they'd parked to reach where the trail went onto Stoner's property. "Now we'll go back in the other direction to see if we can figure out where Gustafsson breaks off of the public trail."

"How will we know?"

"Guess work," Denise admitted. "We've got a couple more hours of daylight. We'll do the best we can."

She turned the snowmobile around and headed back in a northerly direction. When they reached the point where they'd met up with the logging road, Denise stopped to consider their options. She decided to continue north, rather than going west, which would have taken them away from the highway. When they reached the next intersection, she stopped and inspected the trail.

"It doesn't look like anyone's been on that one for a week or so," she said pointing to a branch of the trail that went west. "Let's keep going north."

Ten minutes later they came to another intersection. This time the more traveled trail went off to the east. "I'm betting this is Gustafsson," she said. "It seems whoever came this way was pulling something. See how the center area is smoothed down?"

Bernard didn't know what he was looking at, but he had to trust Denise at that point. He had been cold when they started, but now his teeth were beginning to chatter. "Can we stop for some hot cocoa?"

Fortunately, Denise had decided to stop at the nearby Stewart's to purchase gas and a thermos, which she filled with hot chocolate. She left the machine running, but opened the saddlebag and took out the thermos and two paper cups.

"Yum," Bernard said, after taking a sip. "That's heaven."

"I should have gotten some energy bars, too." Denise mumbled.

"Why? How much longer are we going to be out here?"

She shrugged. "That depends on how far we have to follow this trail. I doubt it'll be more than half an hour before we know if we're following Gustafsson or someone else."

"Won't it be getting dark by the time we head back?"

"That's what these are for," Denise said turning on the snowmobile's headlights.

"Gee. These snowmobile manufacturers thought of everything."

The easterly trail was wide and fairly flat. Denise steered them along the trail slowing down every so often to check the ground in front of them. The afternoon sun was disappearing fast and Bernard was starting to get cold again. Then they came upon another intersection.

"Probably neighborhood kids," Denise remarked pointing to the tracks that went off in various directions. "We'll have to follow them one by one to see if we can pick up the one that belongs to Gustafsson."

They tried one for one hundred yards, but Denise didn't like it. "Not this one."

The next one also failed to be what she was looking

for. The third trail was a charm. "This is it," she yelled back to Bernard.

"Okay." he replied, not knowing if she heard him. He was beginning to recognize the trail features that she was looking for––the smoothed out track in between the tracks left by the machine's runners.

The trail went on for another ten minutes before it diverged again.

"Look at this," Denise said pointing to a trail that broke off the main route over a bank into the woods. "This looks like it was created recently."

Bernard recognized the flattened down area between the sled tracks that Denise said meant something was being pulled behind the snowmobile.

"We'll have to be cautious," she said.

Denise drove their machine onto the new trail. She went along slowly studying the area ahead of them. After five minutes, they came out of the woods into an open field. "Look," she said. The trail headed towards an old barn.

Denise eased the machine forward at a slow pace. "Let me know if you spot anyone," she told Bernard.

She stopped when they reached the front of the barn and turned off the machine. "Look. Footprints."

Indeed, there were boot prints in the snow around the front of the barn.

"Someone stopped here," she said, "then went on…without whatever they were pulling."

"Why stop here?" Bernard asked.

"That's what we're about to find out," Denise replied.

Peter G. Pollak

Chapter Forty-Four

(5:00 P.M., Same Day)

Logan thought he heard a snowmobile. His captor must be returning. Gustafsson told him when he'd left him in the old barn that when he returned it would be to take Logan deep into the woods where he would leave him to die. Logan was beyond caring. He'd even tolerated the spread of darkness that came with the passage of the day without the panicky feelings he'd suffered recently––feelings he traced to being locked in the isolation cell at Stoner.

When you're about to die, being in the dark didn't strike fear in his heart as much as it had every night after being released from the brightly lit rooms and halls of the Gloversville hospital.

Using a heavy chain, Gustafsson had secured Logan to one of the large four-by-four posts that extended to the barn's ceiling. His hands were attached to the chain by metal handcuffs instead of the plastic straps Gustafsson had used in the past. The chain was loose enough so that Logan could stand and walk around the post or sit down, but that was it.

His captor had left him in the ill-fitting snowsuit that he'd forced him to put on in the basement cell at Stoner, but the cold seeped in anyway. He tried to keep warm by walking around the post. When he got tired, he started walking in place and when he couldn't keep that up, he stood shifting his weight from one foot to the other. At one point he stumbled to one knee. He'd fallen asleep on his feet.

Putting it off as long as possible, Logan ate the egg-salad sandwiches and drank the water Gustafsson had left him. After that he'd dozed on and off. He didn't know what time it was and although his eyes had adjusted somewhat to the darkness inside the barn, there was nothing to see that gave him any hope.

One time when he woke up he realized his hands and feet had started to go numb. He stomped his feet and rubbed his hands together. What if a miracle occurred and he survived? He had to keep a ray of hope alive.

Logan heard the barn door slide open. This must be the end.

He heard voices. Neither sounded like Gustafsson.

"There," someone said. "Isn't that a person?"

"I think its Mac." Someone was running towards him. "Mac! Mac! Is that you?"

Denise? It couldn't be.

"Oh my God, Mac. What have they done to you?"

It was Denise. She squatted down beside him and took off her gloves to feel his face. "He's alive, but he could be suffering from hypothermia. Get the cocoa," she said to the person who was standing behind her.

It looked like Bernard Floer.

"Mac. Say something," Denise said. "We're here. You're going to be okay."

"Am I dreaming?" Logan asked, his lips so cracked he could hardly speak.

"It's us. We found you. We'll get you out of here."

The second person returned.

"Bernard?" Logan asked.

"It's me buddy," Bernard replied. "You've got to

stop putting yourself in these situations. I don't know how many more times I can rescue you."

Logan tried to laugh. But then he remembered he was securely chained to the barn post and that his captor wasn't likely to hand over the key.

Bernard surveyed the situation while Denise fed sips of hot cocoa to the man she knew as Mac Johnson. "How are we going to get him out of here, Denise?"

Without the key to the lock or the handcuffs, they would need a chain saw to cut through the post and hope the barn wouldn't collapse in on them in the process.

"Call the State Police," Denise said. "You must have their number on your cell."

"Great idea," Bernard replied. "Why didn't I think of that!"

He unzipped his snowsuit and extracted his cell phone. Good. He had programmed Lt. Sheridan's number into his phone. He hit dial and waited for the connection. It was taking a long time. "Come on." Still no connection. He returned to the home screen. "No service," he said.

"What? Shit," Denise said. "Who's your carrier?"

"Verizon?"

"Mine's ATT." She stood up and retrieved her cell from an inside pocket. "Damn. Zero bars."

"Now what?" Bernard asked.

Denise looked panicky. "We've got to get help."

"You go," Bernard said. "I'll stay here. Leave me the flashlight and some blankets."

"Are you sure?" she asked.

"Someone's got to stay with Mac."

Denise nodded. "Okay. I'll go back to my car. If

there's still no service, I may have to drive all the way to Meadow Lake before I hit a cell tower."

"What about stopping at Stoner and asking to use their phone?" Bernard asked.

"If they're behind this, they're not going to let me--"

"Don't tell them. Pretend you're having car trouble."

"It's too risky," she said. "I'll hurry."

Bernard nodded. "Okay. Go."

"Hang in there, Mac," Denise said. "We're going to get you out of this."

"Bring back the cavalry," Bernard told her.

"Come get the blankets," Denise told him.

Bernard walked with her out to the snowmobile.

She gave him the two blankets that came with the machine and the large flashlight. "Here's a first aid kit," she said. "It may come in handy."

Bernard took the supplies. "Good. Go. You've got to get back here before whoever put Mac here returns."

Chapter Forty-Five

(5:30 P.M., Same Day)

The hot cocoa and the presence of his friends gave Logan a ray of hope. Bernard came back into the barn. He helped Logan to his feet. Logan felt light-headed, but the cocoa gave him a little energy boost. He walked around the post in circles a bit for a while, but soon got tired. Now they were sitting and talking. Logan knew Bernard was trying to keep him from falling asleep, but he was extremely tired.

Bernard threatened to start a fire in the barn to warm them up. Logan was relieved when Bernard admitted that might be a bad idea.

"I guess a fire on a wood floor would be hard to control," Bernard said laughing.

Logan nodded. "Not to mention the smoke might--"

"Oh, you're right. The wrong person might see it and get here before the good guys."

"What's that?" Logan asked pointing to a red cloth bag with a white cross on it.

"Oh," Bernard said. "I almost forgot. Denise gave me the first aid kit that came on the snowmobile. Let's see what's inside."

Just then Logan heard a snowmobile. He didn't know how long Denise had been gone. *What if it was Gustafsson?* "Hide," he told Bernard.

Bernard stood up and faced the front of the barn. Someone slid the front door open and shined a bright light in their eyes.

"Whoa. What have we here?"

Logan recognized Paul Gustafsson's voice.

"Who are you?" Bernard demanded.

Gustafsson came into the barn. "I could ask the same thing about you."

"I'm not telling you anything until you tell me who you are and what your business is," Bernard replied.

Gustafsson came closer. "You want to know my business? It's dealing with punks like you."

Bernard stepped in front of Logan. "You must be the one who kidnapped my friend here. I demand that you release him immediately."

Gustafsson raised the flashlight temporarily blinding Bernard. "You're mighty brave for someone who's out here in the middle of nowhere. How's your cell phone working by the way?"

"My partner went to get the State Police," Bernard said. "They'll be here any minute. Things will go better for you if you give up now."

Gustafsson pushed Bernard in the chest with his light. "Is that right? That's very big of you."

"Stop that," Bernard said. "Unless you want to add assault to the charges you're already facing."

Gustafsson pushed him again. When Bernard raised his arms to defend himself, Gustafsson swung the flashlight catching Bernard on the side of the head and knocking him to the floor. "Assault is the least of your troubles, buddy." He leaned over Bernard and hit him once more in the back of the head.

"Enough," Logan yelled.

"Another country heard from," Gustafsson said laughing. He raised the flashlight as if to strike Logan who flinched. "Looks like I've got two bodies to dispose of."

Gustafsson dragged Bernard by the feet out of the barn. A few minutes later he came back for Logan. He opened the chain lock and lifted Logan up with one arm and shoved him towards the barn door. Logan fell on his face.

"Looks like I've got to drag you too," Gustafsson mumbled. He grabbed Logan by the feet and dragged him out the door his head banging on the floor and then the snow. His captor lifted Logan and threw him on top of Bernard Floer's prone body. He felt himself being tied onto the toboggan Gustafsson had used to transport him from Stoner to the barn.

"Time for another little ride," Gustafsson said, starting up his machine.

Peter G. Pollak

Chapter Forty-Six

(6:00 P.M., Same Day)

Logan shifted his body to try to assess Bernard's condition. The photographer moaned occasionally with the bouncing of the toboggan, but was still unconscious. Logan felt something bulky inside Bernard's snowsuit. He worked one arm free and managed to unzip the front of Bernard's snowsuit. It was a digital camera. Logan didn't know precisely how to work it, nor did he know what good it would do. Maybe he could take some photos that could later be used to prove Gustafsson's guilt.

No more than fifteen minutes had passed when Logan heard a strange noise. It was getting louder. A helicopter! *It must be the State Police! Denise was able to contact them!*

Gustafsson must have heard it also because he slowed the snowmobile down, then brought it to a full stop. He turned off the headlights.

The helicopter was almost overhead. They'll never see us in the dark Logan realized. He brought the camera close to his face trying to figure out how to turn it on. He punched each button in turn. He must have hit the right button because the camera suddenly came to life.

Logan reached through the ropes, holding the camera as high as he could and pushed what he hoped was the shutter button. A flash went off. He pushed it again, and then again.

Suddenly the camera was knocked out of his hand. Gustafsson had noticed the flashes. "None of that. You're more trouble than you're worth."

Had the people in the helicopter seen the flashes? They didn't seem to be getting any closer. In fact they seemed to be moving farther away. "Help," Logan yelled. "Help."

He felt a blow to the back of his head. Then darkness.

He smelled gasoline. Where am I? Cold. Pain. His head hurt. Logan opened his eyes and looked around. He was lying against a tree in the middle of a snow bank. He was no longer wearing the snowsuit Gustafsson had stuffed him into nor was he wearing either gloves or boots. Bernard Floer was nearby propped against a large tree. His snowsuit and boots had also been removed. His eyes were closed.

A few yards away on the snowmobile trail Paul Gustafsson was pouring gasoline into the snowmobile tank from a large red plastic container.

He must have finished gassing up, because he closed the spare can and put it back in the storage area under the seat. He saw that Logan had regained consciousness.

"Awake again," he said to Logan. "Good. I want you to see what's happening. This is where I say goodbye, but don't count on walking out of here alive. You'll never make your way back before the cold gets to you and don't count on your buddies finding you. That helicopter you heard––it's long gone. They never spotted us."

"You don't want to do this," Logan said. "Give yourself up."

"Don't be ridiculous," Gustafsson said, laughing. "That's not happening."

"It's life in prison if we die."

"I'll take my chances."

Logan couldn't think of anything else to say that had a chance of convincing Gustafsson to give himself up.

"I could have left you tied you up," Gustafsson said, "but that would conflict with the story I'm going to tell the authorities when they ask me if I had a role in any of this. Get this. I'm going to tell them that you and your buddy here wandered off by yourselves and must have gotten lost."

"Without boots? That won't wash and you know it," Logan yelled as Gustafsson started the snowmobile.

"Maybe, maybe not," Gustafsson said. He seemed to consider Logan's comment; then he reached into the storage compartment on the back of the snowmobile and took out both pair of boots and threw them into the woods on the other side of the trail. "Don't say I never did anything for you."

Gustafsson turned the snowmobile around and, without giving Logan a last look, drove off. As the lights and sound of his machine diminished, Logan was left in the blackness and quiet of the wintry forest.

He had to find those boots. He tried to stand, but his stocking feet sank deep into the snow. Half walking, half crawling he forced himself towards where he thought the boots would be. After reaching the packed down snowmobile trail, he stood up. He couldn't see the boots in the dark.

It was futile. His feet were numb. Why not just give up? It would be over soon.

He remembered the helicopter. He had tried to attract its attention with Bernard's camera, but it was not likely that they'd seen the flashes. Maybe it wasn't the state police, but rather a helicopter on some other business. But what if Denise had reached the State Police? She wouldn't give up. She'd keep looking until she found him. He had to try to stay alive––for her sake.

Logan's eyes adjusted somewhat to the darkness. Looking around again he saw what might be a boot. He crawled forward. Success! He put it on. Where were the others? He saw a second one nearby; then saw a third, back towards the trail.

He put on two matching boots, doing the best he could to knock the snow off his socks which were caked with icy snow. He pushed himself to his feet. He saw the fourth boot partially submerged in the snow.

Bernard! He had to help him.

He walked back through the deep snow to where Gustafsson had left the photographer. He hadn't regained consciousness. His skin was cold. His body temperature was already dangerously low. Logan knelt down to pull Bernard over to the snowmobile trail where he'd left the extra boots. He felt something bulky in his snowsuit pocket. Logan reached inside. It was the first aid kit from the snowmobile. Bernard must have stuffed it into his pocket when Gustafsson came into the barn.

He put the boots on Bernard and opened the kit. Maybe there was something in it that would help them keep alive.

Logan heard a snowmobile approaching. It sounded like more than one. Someone had seen the light stick he found in the first aid kit that was now burning brightly in the middle of the snow-packed trail.

Peter G. Pollak

The first snowmobile came around the bend its headlights blinding him. The machine skidded to a stop almost knocking him over.

Denise Richardson leapt off the machine and grabbed him in her arms.

Peter G. Pollak

Chapter Forty-Seven

(Noon, Friday, February 3, 2006)

Opening his eyes Logan knew he was in a hospital room. When he saw Denise Richardson standing beside his bed, he wondered if he was back in Nathan Littauer Hospital in Gloversville. That thought made him laugh despite the pain searing every part of his body.

"What's so funny?" Denise asked, clearly amazed at her friend's demeanor.

"It must be ground-hog's day," Logan managed to say.

Two days later Logan woke to discover a crowd of people standing around his hospital bed. Denise was there, as was Dr. Bhatt and Lt. Sheridan, the State Police lieutenant who had interviewed him after his first rescue.

"Mr. Gifford?" Lt. Sheridan said. "I hesitate to ask you how you feel."

Logan wet his lips. "I'm almost getting used to this."

"Well, once again I have some questions for you, but first I'd like to introduce you to Agent Seagram of the FBI."

A tall thin man in a dark suit stepped forward and gave Logan a half-salute. "That's me. I hope you're up to talking because I'm sure you'll have a lot of interesting things to tell us."

"I'll do my best," Logan replied.

"You've got a visitor," the duty nurse told Logan three days later. In walked Bernard Floer with another man behind him. Bernard was in street clothes but had a bandage around his head.

"They're releasing me today," Bernard told Logan. "So I thought I'd come and see how you're doing."

Logan shook his head. "I'd like to say something humorous, but I'm all out of jokes at the moment."

"I can understand. You've had quite a run of bad luck."

"Bad luck or bad karma––whatever the cause I hope it's about to change."

Floer nodded. "You bet it is. The people who tried to kill you can't hurt you now. Denise tells me they're all behind bars."

Logan shook his head. "I think we beat them, the three of us. So, how are you feeling?"

Bernard touched the bandage on his head. "Still a little sore, but I'm a fast healer. Thanks for saving my life by the way."

After Logan lit the fire stick which he found in the first-aide kit, he used the smelling salts to revive Bernard and then opened a package of body warmers, which he used to warm their hands while they sat on the snowmobile trail praying that someone would see the light before it went out.

"I still owe you one," Logan said.

Bernard laughed. "By the way, this is my friend Thomas Flowers. He'd like us to stop meeting this way."

That brought a laugh from both Logan and Flowers.

"Tell him the next time we meet it's going to be to celebrate," Logan said.

"I know the perfect place," Flowers said "--a restaurant down our way that serves great food and has a wine cellar to die for."

Logan smiled. "As long as it's the opposite direction from Desolation Ridge, I'll be there."

Logan was released from the hospital two days later. He was pleased that Denise Richardson came in to help him get checked out even though she wasn't on duty.

"Let me see how you look," she said as he emerged from the bathroom.

"Better than the last time I was released?"

"A lot better. That suit fits you fine, but here, let me help you with the tie."

Logan's hands were still not fully recovered from the frostbite he'd suffered from spending more than eight hours in the abandoned barn and another sitting in the middle of the snowmobile trail.

Denise straightened his tie. "Are you sure you want to come back to Gloversville after this is over?"

Logan nodded. "Positive. I've got nothing waiting for me anymore in Connecticut."

As a result of learning his identity, Logan had contacted his family only to discover that his wife, believing him guilty of the crime to which he'd been forced to confess and also that he'd committed suicide, filed for divorce and had remarried. When he spoke with her by phone, however, she agreed to let him get reacquainted with his daughters. Although he looked forward to spending time with them, he didn't want to live in Connecticut amidst all the upper middle class families commuting to their city jobs and car-pooling to their ballet lessons and soccer practices.

Gloversville offered a different kind of life. One that was more and more appealing to him as he discussed the possibility with Denise and other people on the hospital staff. It was also a place he felt he could bring his daughters to visit during school and summer vacations.

"I think you'll find things will go a little better for you this time," Denise said.

"They will if you invite me to dinner and cook some more of that eggplant parm," Logan said.

"It's a deal. Now go knock 'em dead."

Logan sat down in the wheel chair and let Denise push him through the hospital corridors to the front door where FBI agent Seagram was waiting to drive him to Albany. There they'd board a flight to Washington, D.C. The following day he was scheduled to be the star witness in a Congressional hearing on the unethical business dealings of Congressman Clarence Best, with kickbacks from Tekram Corp. as one example.

Tekram's CEO and Chief of Security were behind bars awaiting trial on multiple charges, as were Dr. Plentikov, Stoner Sanitarium's Chief Medical Officer, and Paul Gustafsson, Stoner's Security Chief.

Seagram warned him that he'd be a busy man over the next six months testifying in criminal trials, but he told him not to worry––either the FBI or New York State Police would provide security for him on each of those occasions.

Logan wasn't worried. He'd been left for dead twice. All he wanted to think about now was living.

-30-

20275755R00129

Made in the USA
Charleston, SC
03 July 2013